AN ALARMING SCIENCE FICTION NOVEL

NOAH'S ARK II:

*Annihilation and revival of
the Human Race*

DR. Z. GILEAD

Author of "The Architects of Doom"; "soma"; The Djinn of the Ring"

NOAH'S ARK II: ANNIHILATION AND REVIVAL OF THE HUMAN RACE
AN ALARMING SCIENCE FICTION NOVEL

iUniverse books may be ordered through booksellers or by contacting:

iUniverse
1663 Liberty Drive
Bloomington, IN 47403
www.iuniverse.com
844-349-9409

ISBN: 978-1-6632-2973-1 (sc)
ISBN: 978-1-6632-2974-8 (hc)
ISBN: 978-1-6632-2975-5 (e)

Library of Congress Control Number: 2021920247

Print information available on the last page.

iUniverse rev. date: 11/08/2021

Dedicated to my lyricist brother, Ilan Goldhirsh
Who wished only the best to all people

INTRODUCTION

Nowadays, most of us and not only Englishmen, often talk about the weather and our climate. We sit at night in front of our TV sets, and various meteorologists and environmental experts tell us that our planet is rapidly **heating up** and **drying up,** because of the effect of the men-made greenhouse gases. The meteorologists and environmental experts claim that these calamities are but an introduction to two imminent and much worse catastrophes:

1. Our planet's supplies of drinking water are rapidly dwindling due to a very dangerous decrease in rain falls. As a result, we are suffering from droughts, in most areas of the world which also seriously damage food production.

2. Glaciers and snow in the world are melting and are raising the levels of the oceans. Several Coastal cities are already being flooded, and soon our whole world will drown.

We hear these warnings of the climatologists with trepidation but leave the fight against the culprit greenhouse gases to our heads of state. They signed at least two treaties against the world's gas pollution but implemented them very feebly. If **they** fail their duty to the world, what can **we**, ordinary citizens do to ward off the danger? Therefore, we shrug our shoulders hopelessly, nervously chew our fingernails and continue with our mundane lives.

However, I, a retired scientist, fearing for the fate of my children and grandchildren, could not remain idle. I decided to join the fight against the greenhouse gases to the best of my ability, however small it may be. I planned to write an extremely alarming Science Fiction novel that will scare my readers and cause at least them to join the protest marches against the irresponsible neglect of our politicians. Short of mutinying against our current leaders, we can only demonstrate and march!

However, in the middle of my writing, I began to waver … Are the climatologists' predictions of our planet's future demise accurate? Perhaps they are they just "fake" warnings, as President Trump claims? During research for my novel, I read an assessment report on our climate in the *"Intergovernmental Panel on Climate Change,"* a scientific and inter-governmental body under the auspices of the United Nations. This panel stated that satellite- and sea- level gauges in islands of the Pacific Ocean do indeed show a rise in sea levels. Fortunately, the report said, this rise is small, and does not exceed the regular *up-and-down* swing of the heights measured in recent years. This report did a lot to alleviate my fears of the future of my descendants and made me stop writing.

Despite that reassuring report, I continued with my Internet search. Regrettably, I found a worrying article in the December 2017 issue of ***the National Oceanic and Atmospheric Administration of the US Department of Commerce.*** This article stated that global sea levels have been rising over the past century, and that **the rate of rising had increased in recent decades**. In 2014, for instance, the global sea level was 2.6 inches above the 1993 average. Moreover, the article stated, sea levels continue to rise at a rate of about one-eighth of an inch per year.

In addition, I read a ***National Geographic*** report, issued at the end of December 2017 that stated the following: "Tide gauge readings and satellite measurements tell us that over the past century, the global mean sea level had risen by 4 to 8 inches (10 to 20 centimeters). Moreover, the annual rate of rising over the past 20 years has been 0.13 inches (3.2 millimeters) a year, **roughly twice the average speed** of the preceding 80 years."

True, the rise in sea levels described above appear to be trivial, but I continued my studies further, and saw a series of articles that appeared in the **Washington Post.** These articles cited new scientific evidence that proved that the melting of the glaciers accelerates faster than anyone thought previously. This dire prediction did not remain without support. It was followed by similar warnings that appeared in several additional newspapers and climatological journals.

More recent reports such as that issued by the National Aeronautics and space administration (NASA), say that the sea levels have risen about 6.7 inches in the last century and the rate of increase doubled in the last decade. Due to the rising global temperatures, oceans tend to absorb a lot of heat and these increased temperatures of water lead to destructive and stronger weather patterns such and the current calamities that our planet is heaping on us: Tornadoes, Tsunamis, earthquakes, and much more.

The Environmental Protection Agency of the federal government of the USA recently published data that says that the concentration of greenhouse gases from human activities increased by 35 percent from 1990 to 2010. Emissions of carbon dioxide, which account for about three-fourths of total emissions, increased by 42 percent over this period. Carbon dioxide in the atmosphere caused a Climate forcing, which is a change in the Earth's energy balance, leading to either a warming or cooling effect over time. An increase in the atmospheric concentrations of greenhouse gases produced a positive climate forcing – a warming effect. From 1990 to 2015, the total warming effect from greenhouse gases added by humans to the Earth's atmosphere, increased by 37 percent leading to our present weather calamities.

Consequently, I decided to complete the writing of my alarming SF novel and to try to publish it in the hope that it may persuade the readers to join the millions who are now inspired by the Swedish teenage activist Greta Thunberg and protest in the social network against the gas pollution. Unfortunately, the Corona plague nowadays curbs more impressive protesting...

CONTENTS

BOOK 1

BATTLE PROPOSALS

CHAPTER 1

Enlistment of Tycoons to Help the Climate's Victims

ohn Roberts, the spokesman of the new Noah's Ark organization, sat tired but satisfied in front of his computer. He had just completed twenty-four hours of feverish writing. His ashtray was full of cigarette stubs, and his garbage basket contained eight empty coffee cups that he had drawn from the coffee machine in his office. He had successfully completed an important task that was assigned to him by Bill Just and Walt Beaufort, the co-chairmen of **"Noah's Ark" Organization.** He wrote for them two stirring addresses that they would present in an important fund-raising meeting that they had instigated. When he started writing he did not know much about the current frightening weather problem. Therefore, he had to refer to the google to compensate for his ignorance.

His two bosses were very famous because of their

philanthropic enterprises, and now they intended to start a new enterprise: a fight against the greenhouse gases. The name of their new Organization was meant to imply fear from an imminent flood, like the one that Noah had to face in the Old Testament's story: *"But Noah found grace in the eyes of the Lord. And God said unto Noah: The end of all flesh is come before me; and behold, I will destroy the whole earth"* *(Genesis 6).*

Another task that Roberts had already completed in the preceding two weeks was also successful. He contacted many of the world's wealthiest tycoons and invited them to the "fund-raising meeting". Most of the tycoons that he had contacted agreed to participate in the meeting. While they had been envious of Bill Just and Walt Beaufort for their financial abilities, they also respected them for their philanthropic work. Most of them realized that Just and Beaufort planned to enlist their support to help the climate's victims. Not all the invited tycoons were selfless enough to help the climate's victims by their own initiative. However, their businesses suffered from the climate's effects and therefore they agreed to participate in the meeting and were ready to do their share of relief work.

The meeting was going to take place via simultaneous tele-presence with multifaceted Skype screen. Before the start of the conference, the broadcasting screens were quickly installed in the offices of the participating tycoons. Each screen was labeled at its bottom with the name of its occupant. Some of the tycoons, due to different time zones, had to stay awake at night for the meeting. At the prearranged time, all screens came alive. Bill Just's visage appeared in his screen, and he started the meeting.

First, he thanked all the participants for their agreement to attend, and then, without further delay, he came straight to the matter at hand:

"Dear honorable friends,

All of you are aware that our planet's climate in our past year of 2022 was a very bad one—the worst yet in all the recorded climatological history. Moreover, it came in the wake of three years, each of which was worse than the preceding one.

I am sure that all of you know that the climatic disasters we are facing are because of the greenhouse gases in our troposphere. These gases had already caused and continue to generate—with a quick escalation—disasters that are quickly destroying our world. Let me enumerate them briefly.

Most of the areas of our world suffer from very hot weather. The oceans, our soil, and the air in our troposphere are heating up (*The troposphere is the ten mile air layer closest to our ground*). The heating rate the soil and air, may seem to be trivial, but it is constantly rising. Thus, between 1906 and 2005, the average world's air temperature rose by 0.74 degrees Celsius. Additionally, according to several extrapolations, just five years from today, it will be higher than our current air temperature by up to 1.5 degrees. That may not seem serious, right? Wrong! This is extremely serious because the temperatures of our oceans are increasing even faster and are already causing a fast thawing of glaciers in the poles with a resulting rise in sea levels! The shores of several lowland countries are already flooded, and within a few more years, seawater will submerge the whole earth—except for the high mountaintops!

Moreover, our planet is heating up and terrible droughts exist in many countries! Rains are considerably scarcer now, and whatever rains that do fall, are torrential and cover small areas only. In the last three years for instance, 40 to 50 percent of the area of the USA did not receive any rain, and the situation in other continents is not any better. This year, tens of thousands of farmers in drought-stricken India committed suicide because they could not support their families. The photographs of their corpses appeared without any respect for the dead, on most news websites.

Food production is reduced due the ever-changing schedules of raining that create havoc in the program of plowing, seeding, and planting. and sowing. The droughts also caused an increased pumping of water from wells. This pumping had already depleted the underground aquifers severely. As of today, a full third of the world's most significant aquifers show a great loss of stored water.

In addition, huge blazes occur in the rainforests because of the increased air temperatures and the droughts. These blazes had already annihilated large regions of the forests that used to supply oxygen by photosynthesis. Moreover, in addition to the fires in the rainforests, callous timber cutting for building and for the exposure of soil for agriculture, further decimated the forests. This great reduction in photosynthesis increased the concentration of carbon dioxide, one of the greenhouse gases, in our troposphere! Due to the scarcity of photosynthesis, Carbon dioxide is not anymore transformed into oxygen and glucose.

To add insult to injury, floods, hurricanes, typhoons, cyclones, tornadoes, and tsunamis occur at a higher frequency than that which had been reported throughout our whole history. Since the sea levels rose because of the thawing of glaciers, storms that start in the seas are drawing greater volumes of seawater for their devastating routes inland. In addition, gusts of violent windstorms swirl up vast amounts of dust from our soil and are causing a thinning of the earth's fertile topsoil, which even in normal times is only a few feet thick.

Most of you probably know that Walt Beaufort and I established, several years ago, a welfare organization that had helped hundreds of thousands of poor people and climate victims on several continents. We fed the poor, transferred climate victims to camps on safe ground, and supplied all their existence needs.

Recently, however, we began to realize that our work is hopeless and is nothing more than a drop in a bucket. We resemble the young boy in the famous Dutch story who passed a dam that had sprung a small leak that threatened to grow and destroy the dam. He put his finger in the hole to prevent the dam from collapsing until somebody came and called for help.

The boy in the Dutch story succeeded in averting a catastrophe. However, Walt and I are unable to cover the climate's "hole." Nowadays, we manage to help only a small percentage of the rapidly growing number of poor people and climate refugees.

Therefore, Walt and I decided to change direction and wage an aggressive preventive war against the greenhouse gases. For this purpose, we established a non-profit organization called **Noah's Ark** and hired numerous scientists who devised various proposals to eliminate greenhouse gases. I will not describe these proposals just now. You will soon receive descriptions of the proposals, one by one, as they start operation.

The name of **Noah's Ark** was chosen at the suggestion of one of our advisers, who is familiar with the Old Testament. **Noah's Ark** is the name assigned in the sixth chapter of Genesis to a rescue vessel built by Noah, the only honest and charitable person in his generation. When Noah finished building the ark, he entered it with his family and pairs of all animal species in the world. Because humanity, other than Noah, had become corrupt and merciless, God brought a flood to the world, and all other humans and animals drowned.

Similarly, humankind has also now became corrupt. We are damaging the delicate climate's equilibrium on our earth by contaminating our atmosphere with anthropogenic greenhouse gases that are produced by the burning of various fossil fuels. This practice, which started with the industrial revolution, is heavily loading our atmosphere with damaging gases.

In biblical times, God pitied Noah and saved him and his family from the deluge. Now, *again* a vast deluge is coming to our world. But apparently, there is no God to pity us and to save us. Only strong gas-eliminating measures can save humanity!

It is not the purpose of Walt and me to compare ourselves to Noah's God. However, with our scientists, we will try to put an end to the devastations of our climate by an eradication of greenhouse gases. We hope that the proposals that we had devised will eliminate most of the gases and tame our climate. For this purpose, we have six consecutive proposals in our arsenal. Each proposal will be activated if its predecessor, God forbid, fails. The proposals are numbered from Noah's Ark proposal 1 to Noah's Ark proposal 6. Proposal 6, should it be activated, will eliminate greenhouse gases with a new, powerful explosive that our physicists are going to produce.

I like to read science-fiction novels in which all countries in our world stopped their territorial conflicts and united to fight against galactic invaders. Now, a *new* invader, armed with photons (heat) from our sun, threatens our world! Fortunately, the general world- peace that now exists, will permit us to implement all our proposals, since they require global cooperation.

Walt and I wish to emphasize that we were not asked by the United World Government to act, nor are we driven by a "Messiah Complex..." We are just acting as concerned citizens who had succeeded in their financial ventures and felt obliged to help the threatened Humanity.

The "**Noah Ark's**" proposals were chosen to be in such a way that they would not harm any of the populations in the world upon their implementation. We have surveyed the opinions of many populations, and anyway all of them agreed that we should proceed, even at the cost of some inconvenience or discomfort. Also, we presented our proposals to the United World Government and received its wholehearted approval."

Throughout all of Bill Just's speech, a hum of approval was heard from the tycoons - whispers in the style of "Bravo," or "Hurrah," and "way to go". True, the proposals had not been described to them yet, but all of them had complete confidence in Just and Beaufort and their scientific advisers.

When Bill Just finished his speech, a round of applause followed him as he yielded the screen to Beaufort.

Beaufort said: "Dear friends, Bill and I believe that we can finance **all** of "**Noah's Ark's**" six proposals with our own resources. In addition, we can still also continue to finance our welfare organization. However, **to be on the safe side**, we have decided to stop our participation in our welfare organization. Therefore, we have invited all of you to the present meeting. We are hoping that all or most of you may agree to carry the burden of the welfare organization in our stead. We had summarized all the experience and locations' data that we had accumulated during our past work and will transfer them to those who wish to help. We ask all of those who wish to participate, to raise their hands and our secretaries will record their names. Please, open your hearts and purse strings, and all Humanity will bless you!"

Beaufort completed his appeal, and the hands of many tycoons were raised. The Organization's secretaries recorded the names of the volunteering tycoons and sent them the data-packages on the next day. Pleased with the success of the enrollment, Just and Beaufort reclaimed the screen and thanked all the participants. Seconds later, the images on the screen finally dimmed, and disappeared one by one.

CHAPTER 2

The announcement of the establishment
"Noah's Ark's" Organization

On August 20th of the year 2022, a whole-page announcement appeared in all the newspapers whose enrollment was over one million readers. The announcement was translated for the non-English language newspapers by a team of translators who were hired by the Organization on a regular basis. It was also broadcast by major television networks twice daily. **To emphasize the text of the announcement in the various newspapers, it was printed over a colored background.** Those people who still lived in relatively calm areas, in which publication means still existed, admired the wide advertising methods that the Organization employed. An English text of the announcement is shown below:

A model of Noah's Ark in Holland.
Created by Huibers
"Noah's Ark" Organization
A non-profit organization, 1300 NW,
Suite 200E, Washington D.C.

Announcement No. 1: Establishment of a new Organization called *Noah's Ark* which is intended to eradicate the greenhouse gases

08.20.2024

(This announcement was written by the two co-chairmen of the new Organization, Bill Just and Walt Beaufort):

Dear citizens of the world!

We, Walt Beaufort, and I, Bill Just, proclaim here today that we are launching a new Organization. We call this Organization **"Noah's Ark"**.

The aim of this Organization is to remedy the terrible climate's cataclysm which is affecting our whole world these past few years. The name of our organization was derived from chapter 6 of the Old Testament that describes how Noah and his family built a roof-covered boat, i.e., an ark, to escape from a terrible deluge that God brought to the world when humankind corrupted their ways and angered Him. We suffer now from terrible climate onslaughts that had come because we **also corrupted our ways** – we damaged the Climate's equilibrium by contaminating our atmosphere with anthropogenic greenhouse gases produced by the burning of various forms of Fossil Fuels, a practice that started with the entrance of the industrial revolution in the nineteenth century. Fossil fuels contain high percentages of carbon and include petroleum, coal, and natural gas. Other commonly used derivatives include kerosene and propane. Fossil fuels range from volatile materials with low carbon to hydrogen ratios, like methane, to liquids like petroleum, and to solid materials composed of almost pure carbon, like anthracite coal. All the materials that I listed, produce a large volume of carbon dioxide greenhouse gas when they burn.

I am sure that there are many among you who had learned from various media sources that Bill and I had established a large relief organization that helped the poor and the needy populations a few years ago and now is also helping refugees from the climate's cataclysms. Our organization provided food, medicines, and safe lodgings. We had also supplied desalinated water to the citizens of the African continent that now undergoes now a terrible drought. For that purpose, we built desalination plants on the shore of the Red Sea and their water was transported inland by a large pipe-network. We had also helped refugee populations in other continents by sending them medicines, milk powder, and protein concentrates.

As an extension to our past actions, we have decided now to attack the very cause of the terrible climate that we are now facing that is caused by the "blanket" of greenhouse gases that lurks in our atmosphere. Our earth heats up because of the infrared radiation that we receive from the Sun. This heat cannot dissipate back to space because of the gases. This heat is trapped in the troposphere, as if it resides inside the glass walls of a greenhouse that allows the sun to heat its interior but does not permit the heat to escape. Both the air in the atmosphere, our soil, and our oceans heat up, and this causes the terrible climatic events that we are experiencing.

With the help of scientific advisers that we gathered, our new Organization had developed several revolutionary proposals to fight this accumulation of Greenhouse gases. Our proposals had gained a wholehearted approval from our United World Government. These proposals will be described to you in additional announcements that will be circulated before the performance of each proposal. Note however, that at this stage we have decided to withdraw our support from our previous relief organization to dedicate all our finances and whole attention to our new, important project. We had transferred the responsibility for the continued operation of our relief organization to generous volunteer tycoons that we recruited.

The greenhouse gases in our troposphere are mostly water vapor (between 36% to 70%, depending on the location – whether over desert or sea) and Carbon Dioxide (between 9% to 26%). The troposphere also contains much smaller concentrations of Methane, Nitrogen Dioxide, Ozone, and Chloro-Fluoro Carbon. This last gas was used in the past as a propellant in various vaporizers and is very destructive to our Ozone layer. Luckily, it is now banned in most countries, and its concentration in the troposphere is slowly dissipating.

The heat in the troposphere is very dangerous but is also beneficial. Without it, the air temperature over our planet would have been Minus 18 degrees centigrade. Such a freezing temperature would have prevented the growth of all trees and crops, and the appearance of animals and Man.

It had been believed in recent past, that the greenhouse gases only cause a heating of the air in our troposphere. However, it is realized now that the air temperature of the troposphere indeed rises, but the **temperatures** of the **Earth's soil** and the **oceans rise even faster**. This realization was reached when several climatologists checked two climate's components: the air temperature over our globe and the heat radiating back from our planet to space. Using data that was accumulated over several scores of years from Nasa's weather satellites, the scientists had discovered that between the years 1979 to 1995, air temperatures rose slowly, showing at their peak only an average increase of 0.2 degrees centigrade. They also discovered that the back-radiation of the sun's heat from the soil to space remained at a low, stable value. The climatologists Had concluded therefore that most of sun's heat is absorbed by the soil and by the oceans. Measurements of the temperatures of the soil and oceans indeed verified their conclusions. The soil- and ocean temperatures were found to be much higher than the air- temperatures! Moreover, it was found that **the oceans' temperatures are constantly rising now and are thawing glaciers in the poles. As a result, we see emaciated bears floating on**

small pieces of ice in wide seas. This glacier' thaw is already raising the sea levels all over our earth.

The concentration of the greenhouse gases started to rise at the arrival of the Industrial Revolution in the nineteenth century. Its origin is "anthropogenic". That is - it is being produced by us. We are burning large quantities of Fossil fuels such as oil and coal in our factories and in electricity-producing plants. We also operate ever-increasing numbers of machines and cars. Moreover, large areas in the rain forests are burned down to expose land for agriculture and their trees are cut for lumber. We cultivate large herds of cattle that add a lot of gas as a digestive product.

In the past, photosynthesis by trees converted a lot of Carbon Dioxide, one of the main components of greenhouse gases, into glucose, releasing Oxygen in the process. Now this beneficial process is greatly inhibited. Various climatologists have long warned us that we are moving quickly towards extinction of people in two clear stages:

1. Droughts that cause food and water shortage,
2. Drowning by ocean waters.

While it is true that almost all the governments in the world signed the Kyoto and Paris agreements in 1999 and in 2015 and promised to limit the production of greenhouse gases. However, they are not fulfilling their obligations. Moreover, President Trump, on his election, annulled the signature of USA on the climate agreements. Only in the present year, 2024, and very belatedly, all nations reduced their anthropogenic gas production. Unfortunately, the current greenhouse gases concentrations had already reached a critical-mass level that now requires an active program of removal. This is where we come with our "**Noah's Ark**" proposals.

In additional announcements, that we will issue from time to time, we will describe our proposals for combating the greenhouse gases. We solemnly pledge that we will do everything in our power to eliminate the cause of the climate's scourge. We hope that the very first proposal that we will activate, will succeed. If not, we shall continue with subsequent proposals until we are victorious.

Signed: Will Just and Walt Beaufort

"Noah's Ark" Organization

A non-profit organization, 1300 NW,
Suite 200E, Washington D.C.

Announcement No. 2; "Noah's Ark" proposal No. 1: The seeding of Nanoparticles capable of absorbing Carbon Dioxide Gas

(This announcement was written by John Roberts,
the spokesman for "Noah's Ark" Organization)

09,23.24

Dear citizens of the world!

My name is John Roberts, and I had been appointed to the position of spokesman of the **"Noah's Ark"** organization. Previously I had been working in one of Walt Beaufort's companies. Now, as a spokesman for the organization, my task is to act as a liaison between the organization and you people, and to tell you what

"**Noah's Ark**" is planning to do each time. I am very happy that I was selected to this job, since this way I can, in a very small measure, help in the fight against the Climate's onslaughts.

Before the start of each proposal, I will notify you what its guiding principle is, and how it is going to be performed. I may also have to inform you, regretfully, if any of the proposals will fail.

I sincerely hope that I shall not have to describe all the proposals consecutively because of failures, and that the first proposal, that I shall soon describe below will succeed, and will be the only one that I will need to report on.

I was lucky to have the privilege of sitting in all the brain-storming sessions of the Organization for the formulation of our proposals and saw great scientists at work. People like to call scientists "Eggheads," and indeed, I saw how their brains work so hard until fumes came out of them, and the eggs became "hard-boiled ..."

By describing what is going to happen in "**Noah's Ark's**" proposal No. 1, or any other proposal, if necessary, you will become, as it were, "silent partners" in the organization's work.

Here is the description of proposal number No. 1: Our scientists have suggested that we shall use Nanoparticles that are capable of absorbing Carbon Dioxide gas. As you may know by now, this gas is responsible, together with water vapor, for the weather's catastrophe that we now undergo. The gas-absorbing Nanoparticles will be flown to the Troposphere inside guided missiles that will soar up to the height of 10 miles. At this height, they will be dispersed from the missiles by explosion and will slowly drift down to earth, thus covering wide volumes of the Troposphere.

To those who do not know what Nanoparticles are, I shall explain: Nanoparticles are extremely small particles with the sizes of one to several microns (a micron is one-thousandth of a millimeter). They are produced from a variety of chemicals by very modern chemical syntheses that I do not pretend to understand. Nowadays they are used in the production of very strong building materials. In Medicine, they participate in many areas, foremost of which is a very efficient spreading of various drugs in the body.

Here I want to apologize for feeding you with many difficult chemical terms. We could have spared you this annoyance, but the scientists of "**Noah's Ark**" wanted to describe them for other chemists in the world. There may be chemists somewhere in the world who know of even better absorbing Nanoparticles than those that we intend to use now. We shall be happy if they will contact the Organization to relate their experience and advances.

Our scientists proposed to use two types of Nanoparticles:

1. Nanoparticles made of a polymer called "Poly Ethylenimine (PEI in short) which was coated with "burnt" silica" (what that means, I do not know...). They are very easy to produce in vast amounts, and it is important to note, that they can absorb Carbon Dioxide even in the presence of water vapor.

2. If we fail with the coated PEI particles, we shall use a second type of Nanoparticles called "Metalo-Organic Frameworks" (in short: MOF). These Nanoparticles are made of Copper or Zinc that are bound to an organic-chemistry molecule called Carboxyl. Again, the MOF Nanoparticles are also very easy to synthesize in large quantities, and they, too, can absorb Carbon Dioxide in large amounts.

The use of Nanoparticles had already been advocated in Climatological scientific journals for combating the greenhouse gases. However, without indicating any specific type, and without performing any greenhouse gas absorption experiments. As I have mentioned above, the nanoparticles that we shall use, can only absorb Carbon Dioxide and not water vapor. Still, if we can absorb all the Carbon Dioxide or at least a large volume of it, perhaps we shall significantly improve our weather, and the heat from our planet will finally be able to dissipate to space. As mentioned above, the Nanoparticles will be sent to the troposphere inside guided missiles and will be release from them by an explosion.

The missiles that we shall use were developed in the past by the Russians during the "cold war" with the USA and were intended to intercept attacking enemy planes. The first type of missile that had been developed was called "S-25". It was later followed by additional models. Nowadays, there still exist several thousands of "S-75" missiles in the arsenals of several countries. These missiles were sold to these countries by the Russians or were produced by the countries themselves.

To-day, because of the global peace, the missiles are not serviced anymore. However, our organization carried out discussions with the governments of those countries who still possess these missiles and they promised to put the missiles back in service, as soon as possible. The missiles are two-staged, and the top stage that separates from the bottom propelling-stage, can carry several hundred pounds of Nanoparticles. The missiles also possess an electronic guiding system and can fly vertically at an electronic order from the ground. They can easily reach a height of 10 miles and will release the nanoparticles by explosion, as already described above. The explosion will be triggered by an electronic signal from the ground.

Note that if we fail with "Noah's Ark" proposal No. 1, these same still remaining missiles can also be used in "**Noah's Ark's**" proposals No. 2 and No. 3. I must admit that I personally am not very happy with the use of military destructive machines in our fight to eradicate the greenhouse gases. Even among our scientists there are many who, who do not like this use of military hardware. However, we understand that it is necessary to beat the devil with his own weapons. We must be victorious over the greenhouse devil, or else we shall all perish.

Signed: John Roberts, the Organization's spokesman

Operations' Diary of John Roberts
(Top Secret and Private)

08.23.2024

"Dear Diary,

As a boy, oppressed by a cruel stepfather, writing of a diary offered me some amount of solace! Now, as a grown man and a father myself, I'll try to seek consolation by writing a diary again … This need for consolation arose because my new job as **"Noah's Ark"** spokesman is a stressful one - I act as a sole representative of an organization that is vital to billions of people. These people will breathlessly read everything that I write. If the Organization will succeed in its task to eradicate the greenhouse gases, my two bosses will have the pleasure of notifying the whole world of the success, as is right and proper. However, if any, or all, of the organization's proposals will fail, it will be my wretched task to tell the entire world about it!

Now, my dear diary, I will reveal to you a secret: it is a great honor and a privilege to work for my two philanthropic bosses. Both are idealists with lofty aspirations and integrity. However, I hold a certain grudge against Walt Beaufort since he "stole" my wife, and this is how it happened:

After a very successful production year in one of Beaufort's companies in which I had served as a spokesman, the company held a very sumptuous banquet. All the company's employees and their spouses were invited to the banquet which also hosted Beaufort himself. My wife, Jeanie, was the prettiest and sexiest of all wives or girlfriends present, and immediately attracted Beaufort's attention. During the dances I noticed that Beaufort danced only with her and sometimes pressed her, inappropriately, to his body. Beaufort was divorced at the time, and a well-known "Don Juan". Therefore, I came to rescue her from his lecherous grasp by trying to cut in on their dance. However, Jeanie, apparently, did not want to be rescued and instead asked me to bring them cold drinks. When I quickly returned, I caught Beaufort whispering in Jeanie's ear. When he saw me, he broke contact with some embarrassment, and Jeanie blushed. When we came home, I asked Jeanie what Beaufort had whispered. She answered that he, very bluntly, tried to seduce her and she did not put an end to his flirtation, for fear that it might damage my position in my company.

Two weeks after the company's banquet, Beaufort himself phoned me. After voicing some platitudes concerning my health and that of Jeanie's, he came straight to the point. He said that he is looking for an experienced spokesman for a new, very important Organization that he and a colleague are setting up. Generally, he said, his manpower managers do the hiring. But because of the importance and urgency of the task that the new Organization is going to address, he is doing the "head-hunting" himself. He also said that he asked my current CEO for an evaluation of my abilities, and that my boss praised me. He said that a description and goals of the new Organization have not been publicized yet, and that he wants to offer me the job of the spokesman of the new organization. He also added that it is very high-powered one and offers a very high salary and various other benefits given only to CEOs of his other companies. I coughed a little to hide my surprise on hearing his offer, thanked him, and gladly accepted it.

Then Beaufort said that to perform my job properly, I will have to relocate to the organization's headquarters in Washington where all the planning work is carried out. He also revealed to me that the new Organization will be called "Noah's Ark" and will have Bill Just as a co-chairman. It is intended to try to eliminate the greenhouse gases that surround us. He also asked whether Jeanie, my wife, will agree to relocate to Washington. I immediately answered that I am sure that she will, although I was quite sure that she will not, wishing to remain with our children close to her parents.

Moreover, since the banquet, our relationship had inexplicably cooled down: she started to quarrel with me often, and subsequently also barred our bedroom door from me. Therefore, I decided that if she refused to relocate, I will go alone and initiate a trial separation, although it would grieve me considerably to leave my children with their mother. However, I consoled myself that because of my new promised high salary, I will be able to fly and visit them often, although flying had become very expensive and risky, because of the dangerous climate. To my great surprise, Jeanie agreed to relocate, became reconciled with me, and even let me return to our bedroom…

However, after our moving to Washington, Jeanie started to spend long evenings away from home, using several pretexts. I immediately realized the reason and told her that Beaufort is known as a person who often "flies from one flower to another", and that his liaisons never last more than a few months. To my surprise, she told me that Beaufort proposed to marry her, and that she had decided to accept his offer, but waited to let me get settled in my new job. She asked for a divorce that I let her have. In the divorce trial, a judge allowed me equal visiting and parental care rights and Jeanie waived any alimony and child-support payments.

In my first face-to-face meeting with Beaufort after the divorce, I told him that I am not holding any grudge, and that the best of us won, while thinking to myself that the richest one won ... I was certain that Beaufort will not terminate my job, and I was right in this assumption. Moreover, Beaufort transferred to my service a sexy secretary, hinting that she is very "liberal", and admires powerful men. He also offered her a large salary and told her that I am the one who suggested it ... I tested Beaufort's hints when I asked her for a date and found out that Beaufort did not exaggerate with regards to her "qualifications".

As for the chances for a success of "Noah's Ark" proposals to fight the greenhouse gases, I am very pessimistic. I do not believe that we can tame the terrible Climate. However, only to you alone, my diary, I shall reveal my doubts. I shall, of course, hide them from my future announcements for fear that I may lose my excellent job. Also, I do not want to lose my secretary Anna, whom I learned to love and respect. also, my job is rather easy and entails mostly the transfer of the information that I received from the organization's scientists.

With regards to the scientists, I hope that they are brilliant and will succeed in their task. But, to judge from the case of "Noah's Ark" proposal 1, I was quite surprised to watch the childish behavior of the two Nanoparticle scientists. Each one tried to prevent the use of the other's proposal, to be the only one who shall gain the glory of saving the world. I imagine that their competitive behavior is to be expected, but are they brilliant enough to save the world? we will have to wait and see ... I hope that even if proposal number No.1 fails, at least one or more of our scientists' proposals may do their job.

Titanic Report No. 1
Dear Diary,

I am going to heap upon your pages a very heavy burden. I intend to report on the climate's Catastrophes, which I shall call the "Titanic reports", for obvious reasons. I am quite sure that you, as a dumb object, would not demur, if I describe in your pages terrible climate catastrophes, in which I shall also enumerate the numbers of their victims. With regards to the Titanic, if it had existed today, and would have taken the same course it did 120 years ago, it would have survived. Any floating glacier that it would ram today, would be much smaller and spongy because of the thawing action of the warming-up oceans.

I cannot, gushingly, tell the whole world how sad I am for the millions of men, women, and children who are losing now all their possessions, in the least case, or their lives in the worst case. I must be optimistic and encouraging, even though I do not believe that "Noah's Ark" proposals can work. The "blanket" of Greenhouse gases that wraps us is huge: it is 5 miles thick and surrounds the whole circumference of our planet. I hope, however, that by giving vent to my pessimism and frustration by writing in you, I can achieve a small fraction of catharsis from my spiritual condition. This is a condition of a spokesman forced to voice optimism, beneath which lies a strong fear for the future of world, of his children, and of Anna.

Ocean level report: Holland – about 50% of the Dutch population had to flee from their homes and to migrate to higher-level European countries. About 1.5 million people of this displaced population drowned when the dams on the seashore were breached without any warning.

Vietnam – About 30% of the population had to flee from their homes.

Drought report: Almost 50% of the area of the USA (including the large state of California) did not receive any rain in the past 3 years.

Five African nations urgently require transports of food and water: Ethiopia, Somali, Kenya, Tanzania, and Uganda. Also, the South African government had to stop the supply of drinking water to homes because of a great shortage, leaving its populace to fend for themselves!

About 30 percent of the area of India was hit by a drought. Only India's large rivers somewhat alleviated the situation.

"Noah's Ark" Organization
A non-profit organization, 1300 NW,
Suite 200E, Washington D.C

Announcement No. 3; The
failure of proposal no. 1

(This announcement was written by John Roberts,
the spokesman for "Noah's Ark" Organization)

01.12.2025

Dear Citizens of the world,

The most important part of my job as spokesman of the
organization is the need to inform you of the success
or failure of each consecutive "Noah's Ark's" proposal.
I must now sadly report that proposal No. 1 – the use
of nanoparticles, did not perform as expected. A hint
of a possible failure was already obtained upon the
first seeding of an extremely large numbers of the PEI

nanoparticles. The second type of nanoparticles also did not fare any better...

To measure the degree of removal of the Carbon Dioxide gas, our climatologists used a very advanced and accurate analytical method called High Energy, double pulse. Integrated Path Differential Absorption (IPDA LIDAR). It measures simultaneously both greenhouse gases since each of them absorbs laser radiation waves at a different wavelength. The laser radiation rays are emitted from weather satellites, that were sent many years ago to the troposphere by NASA.

Beyond writing like a parrot whatever the scientists dictated to me on the IPDA LIDAR method, I cannot add anything else. All I can add, is that although we seeded very large amounts of the Nanoparticles in the troposphere, both types of nanoparticles only reduced the concentration of Carbon Di-Oxide Greenhouse Gas by a fraction of a percent.

Signed: John Roberts, the organization's spokesman

"Noah's Ark" Organization

A non-profit organization, 1300 NW,
Suite 200E, Washington D.C

Announcement No. 4; Proposal no. 2: the use of Neutron bombs

(This announcement was written by John Roberts, the spokesman for "Noah's Ark" Organization)

01.25.2025

"Dear citizens of the world,

Following the failure of "Noah's Ark" proposal No.1, We are immediately going to start with proposal No. 2 - the use of Neutron bombs. These bombs will be flown inside the same guided missiles that were used in proposal No.1. The missiles will be used also in proposal No. 3, if still needed. Luckily for the world, the use of the missiles and bombs became possible when in 07.21.2023, a general world peace was proclaimed by all nations, in the wake of the terrible Coronavirus plague. This peace was enforced by strict rules and reprisals against any nation who would break it by starting a war or disobeying an edict of the World's Health organization on the Coronavirus. Even the recalcitrant Sunni Muslim nations accepted the peace, while the Shiite Muslim ones first refused, but finally complied, because of the fear of reprisals.

Quite probably, the use of weapons such as the neutron bombs and the missiles may upset those purists among you who will protest their use. However, we do not have any choice – we must utilize various terrible weapons against the monstrous climate that we are facing! Subsequent proposals will use even more lethal weapons in our fight, as you will see if we fail with additional proposals. Proposal No. 6. for instance, will use an awesome energy weapon never seen before. This simply goes to show you that we are not leaving any stone unturned!

Now I shall describe proposal no. 2: As I have already mentioned above, our scientists and military advisers suggested the use of Neutron bombs. These bombs are a type of atomic bombs that are not dangerous to the environment, but only to living organisms. This is going be quite a revolution – to use warfare weapons for the sake of peaceful aims!

The delivery of the Neutron bombs to the stratosphere will be first performed in Russia, that still has a considerable number of "S-75" missiles despite their slight depletion in proposal No.1. The Russians also still have a stock of Neutron bombs. The World Government had demanded that all nations will dismantle them. The Russians also complied with the order, but carried it out sluggishly, because of the high dismantling- and disposal costs of the bombs' radioactive material.

Before describing the bombs themselves, and how they work, I have to explain what a Neutron is: (the information about it was dictated to me by one of the scientists of the organization) – "Neutrons are particles that are present in the nuclei of all atoms. The nucleus, which resides in the center of each atom, is composed of Neutrons that do not possess any electrical charge and an equal number of protons, which possess a positive electrical charge. For every proton in nucleus of the atom, there also exists in the atom's shell a much smaller particle called electron which has a negative charge, thus balancing the positive charge of the protons.

A neutron bomb is an atomic bomb which produces vast surges of Neutrons that spread out in all directions after the explosion. The principle of action of a Neutron Bomb is very similar to that of a "regular" atom bomb. In the explosion of a "regular" atom bomb there exists a flow of high energy neutrons, but they are locked inside the bomb so that their energy is transformed to vast heat and pressure. In contradistinction, most of the neutrons of a neutron bomb are allowed to escape.

Can a Neutron Bomb remove water vapor molecules? Yes. Water is composed of one Oxygen atom and two Hydrogen atoms. The Oxygen and the Hydrogen atoms of water each contain eight protons (two from the Hydrogens and six from the Oxygen) and six neutrons (from the Oxygen only, because Hydrogen does not possess any neutrons). Since Neutrons that are released from the bomb possess high energy and high penetrability, they will bombard the water vapor atoms and create a secondary fan of protons and neutrons which ought to disintegrate the stratosphere's water vapor molecules in a wide area.

Let us all keep our fingers crossed for the success of the neutron bomb of the World Peace (two incongruences in one sentence …!)

Signed: John Roberts, the organization's spokesman.

"Noah's Ark" Organization
A non-profit organization, 1300 NW,
Suite 200E, Washington D.C

Announcement No. 5; "Noah's Ark" proposal No. 2: The failure of neutron bombs to remove water vapor from the troposphere

(This announcement was written by John Roberts, the spokesman for "Noah's Ark" Organization")

07.27.2025

"Dear Citizens of the world,

Because of the need to inform you of the outcome of "Noah's Ark" proposals we, very regretfully, must inform you that proposal No. 2 failed. It removed large volumes from the water vapor "blanket", but the blanket quickly resurrected itself with an in-flow of water molecules from the vicinity. Alas, this is very similar to the air (thunder) that refills a vacuum created by a lightning! However, I beg of you – do not despair. I know that conditions in most area of the world are completely unbearable and result in millions of wounded and drowning people!

Therefore, I guess that my request from you not to despair is hopeless. However, you survivors should know that we still have additional proposals that will have a "bigger clout", and ought to do the job. Pretty soon, we shall inform you of an additional proposal, proposal number 3, that we pin on it a lot of hope on this one.

Signed: John Roberts, the organization's spokesman

Operations' Diary of John Roberts
(Top Secret and Private)

Date: 08.15.25

"Dear Diary,

I am starting to believe that if the rest of "Noah's Ark" proposals will collapse as speedily as proposal No. 1 and 2, my service as a spokesman is going to be short-lived. However,

I do not care about my job. I was not born a spokesman and saying goodbye to "Noah's Ark" does not worry me. My worries center around the world's future and that of my sons, John Junior and Timothy, as well as that of Anna's. I fear that the task of removing the greenhouse gases' blanket, or even a part of it, may be insurmountable.

Titanic report No. 2
<u>Ocean level report:</u>

China – about 4% of the Chinese population had to leave their homes and to migrate inland. This percentage may look like a relatively small one. But, owing to the large population of China, we are talking about 50 million men, women, and children. Also, despite the efforts of the efficient Chinese regime, 10 million of those who migrated, drowned in their flight.

Vietnam – 25% of its population lost their homes, a matter of 23 million people. There is not yet any official count of the dead.

<u>Drought report:</u> Three large countries and one continent joined the circle of drought and hunger: Brazil, Indonesia, Malaysia, and Australia.

I have decided to stop writing my Titanic reports. They cause me too much pain instead of helping me to alleviate it. However. I will just add now one more report, and then desist from writing.

Operations' Diary of John Roberts
(Top Secret and Private)

09.01.2025

"Dear Diary,

The use of Neutron bombs in proposal No. 2, was suggested by a retired 4-star General by the name of Harold Siebly. His addition as a military adviser to the panel of scientists was important because, after all, we are presently **at war** against the greenhouse gases! I do not possess his military expertise, because I was drafted into the US army just before the termination of all wars in the world. However, I pride myself that I possess an above-average intelligence and I always examine things keenly. I estimated that each neutron bomb will, at most, clean a vapor volume of no more than one cubic mile. However, I was sure that the surrounding "blanket" of the greenhouse gases will quickly refill the void, since it is, after all, 5 miles thick and its circumference around our globe is at least 27,000 miles long!

I was present in the planning sessions of the use of the Neutron bombs and tried to "squeak" my humble rational objection, but I was immediately silenced by General Siebly. I was not at all surprised at the failure of the neutron bomb proposal. While it true that we do not possess enough remaining missiles to attack the whole troposphere, General Siebly wisely planned to use bomber planes to drop the bombs in several heights if they would work. However, the failure of the Neutron bombs to clear very large volumes of water vapor from the troposphere, excluded their continued use. Moreover, we do not possess many bombs and they are difficult to produce – most of the radioactive materials necessary for the bombs were sunk into various oceans inside huge hunks of cement.

Anna brought me a lot of happiness. Since my sons also became captivated by her, she came to live with us. I also proposal to ask her to marry me if we succeed in our fight against the Climate.

This time I am refraining from writing any cynical comments and criticisms in my diary. After all, the scientists, and even including General Siebly, are trying their best. I am starting to believe that any derogatory remarks that I previously wrote, stemmed from my disappointment and fear for the fate of my children, for Anna, and of the destiny of the whole world.

The worry and the fear, and the need to report on the failure of one proposal after the other, completely devastated my psyche. I think that before I shall completely cave in, I shall have to search for psychological counseling.

"Noah's Ark" Organization

A non-profit organization, 1300 NW,
Suite 200E, Washington D.C

**Announcement No. 6; "Noah's Ark"
proposal No. 3: The use of Fuel-Air bombs
for the removal of the greenhouse gases.**

(This announcement was written by John
Roberts, the spokesman for "**Noah's Ark**")

30.06.25

"Dear Citizens of the world,

I am writing this announcement with the intention
of letting you know that we are starting to execute
"Noah's Ark" proposal No. 3: use of fuel-air bombs.
The use of these bombs was again suggested by
General Siebly. Fuel-air bombs are another example
of formidable wartime weapon is being converted by

us into a "peaceful weapon" against the scourges of the Climate.

The fuel-air bombs, like in our first two proposals, will be flown inside "S-75" missiles and will be exploded at different heights over Russia. Russia was chosen as a preliminary trial site to see if these bombs can work because it still possesses a small number of missiles and bombs. The number of the missiles that remained would not be sufficient for a complete "mop-up" operation. However, if the preliminary trial will show promise, we proposal to use high altitude bomber- and passenger planes to disperse the bombs. Fuel-Air bombs are very easy to produce in large numbers since the raw materials for them exist in large amounts.

What exactly are Fuel-Air bombs? These bombs contain, in addition to a main load of liquid fuel or in gel-like form, also small aluminum or magnesium flakes that add more intensity to the fire. The bombs also contain two detonators and two explosive charges that explode one after the other. In the first explosion, the fuel is dispersed as a cloud that becomes mixed with air and the greenhouse gases in the air. The second charge ignites the fuel-air-greenhouse gas mixture. The burning of the cloud creates an explosive wave of intense heat and pressure that advances very quickly in a large area. The pressure created reaches

30 atmospheres, and the temperature created reaches 3000 degrees centigrade.

Unlike the case of regular explosive bombs, in which the burning effects start from a center and then spreads, the pressure and high temperature of fuel-air bombs occurs simultaneously throughout the whole volume of the cloud. Some bombs will be triggered to explode in high altitudes where the oxygen that is necessary for burning is too sparse. Therefore, two chemicals will be added to the fuel: Potassium Chlorate and a Manganese oxide catalyst. When these chemicals are heated in the explosion, they produce a lot of Oxygen. The burning time of the fuel-air cloud is long, and the fire dies out very slowly. These effects should turn the bombs into perfect weapons against the greenhouse gases!

Aside from General Siebly who was mentioned in one of our early announcements, there are several military men among the advisers of the organization, and they contribute a lot to our efforts. This goes to show you how methodical were Just and Beaufort when they hired the best possible team for the organization. If we need to execute additional "war" proposals, you will be able to realize this point much better. I talk about "war" proposals because we are indeed in the middle of a war, where our opponents are giants! Giants of Carbon Dioxide and water vapors that conquered our troposphere, and still do not yield the territories that they brazenly conquered!

As indicated above, in the beginning we shall try the bombs in several locations in Russia. If the fuel-air bombs will succeed in getting rid of large volumes of water-vapor, we shall produce many bombs and re-commission high altitude bombers and confiscate passenger planes for their dropping. Those believers among you, please pray to your gods for our and your success!

Signed: John Roberts, the organization's spokesman.

"Noah's Ark" Organization
A non-profit organization, 1300 NW,
Suite 200E, Washington D.C

Announcement No. 7; "Noah's Ark" proposal No. 3: Failure of the use of Fuel-Air bombs for the removal of the greenhouse gases
(This announcement was written by John Roberts, the spokesman for "**Noah's Ark**")

11.27.2025

"Dear Citizens of the world!

As the spokesman of the "Noah Ark's" organization, I must inform you again, with great regret, that proposal No. 3 failed because of the same reason that caused the failure of proposal No. 2. Apparently, it is very difficult to cause a permanent dent in the thick greenhouse layer that surrounds our globe. We may have to resort, eventually, to our most powerful weapon which is certain to succeed - proposal No. 6. But, before we do, we shall still try additional very good proposals that we still possess!

Signed: John Roberts, the organization's spokesman.

Operations' Diary of John Roberts
Top Secret and Private)

Date: 11.28.2023

"Dear Diary,

Despite my announcement in my last note in the diary, in which I decided to stop writing in the diary, I noticed that the stopping of my writing caused me even more anguish than writing. So here I am again!!

I must admit, however, that I think now that the "Noah's Ark's" bosses should have hired a younger spokesman than me to describe each new proposal. Such a person would be more enthusiastic and less pessimistic. But then, perhaps, it is better that I am not the eager enthusiastic type who would cheerfully exaggerate the chances of the success of each proposal. Thus, at least I would not instill any false hopes in my readers, which then would be followed by even greater disappointments after each failure.

As for the failure of proposals No. 2 and No. 3, I must admit that I am somewhat relieved that we are going to stop the e of aggressive weapons for our "peaceful fight". If we had succeeded with them, I would have been overjoyed, of course.

I must, again, praise myself for my perspicacity. I did not really believe that we can destroy the huge volumes of greenhouse gases in our troposphere...

"Noah's Ark" Organization

A non-profit organization, 1300 NW,
Suite 200E, Washington D.C

Announcement No. 6; "Noah's Ark" proposal No. 4: Failure of the use of Anti-aircraft laser guns for the removal of the greenhouse gases

(This announcement was written by John
Roberts, the spokesman for "**Noah's Ark**")

11.27.2025

Given the collapse of proposals No. 1, No. 2, and No. 3, that depended on the limited availability of missiles, the military advisers of the organization decided to use a weapon that does not suffer from this limitation. Therefore, we are moving now to proposal No. 4, in which we are going to use an earthbound defensive weapon - anti-aircraft laser-guns. A "Laser-gun" may sound to you like a fictional hand-weapon used only in SF novels or movies. However, laser guns are real weapons that were developed in the USA as anti-aircraft devices.

The term "LASER" is an acronym for "Light Amplification by Stimulated Emission of Radiation". A laser emits coherent light rays; that is, they have a straight directed path and do not disperse all over. The laser shoots monochromatic rays (that is, of a narrow single wavelength only). Regular light, like from a lightbulb, emits beams in all directions and therefore its rays are not coherent.

We shall use a kind of military lasers which are called "solid state lasers". These military lasers are mobile devices installed on trucks and are operate by a passage of light through a crystal called Yttrium Aluminum garnet (YAG). A garnet is a mineral that contains silicates and is also used as a gemstone. The USA had produced several thousands of these devices which became superfluous when World Peace was established. They were intended to destroy war planes up to the height of 10 miles (which is the thickness our stratosphere and which contains a 5-mile-thick blanket of greenhouse gases starting from the ground up). Lasers also have many peacetime's uses: in the cutting, melting, and fusing of metals, in delicate surgeries, for communication purposes, for accurate measurement of distances, and many more uses.

"Noah's Ark" Organization
A non-profit organization, 1300 NW,
Suite 200E, Washington D.C

Announcement No. 8; "Noah's Ark" proposal No. 4: The failure of the use of anti-aircraft laser-guns
(This announcement was written by John
Roberts, the spokesman for "Noah's Ark")

02.01.2026

"Dear Citizens of the world!

In great sorrow, I must inform you that despite the organization's extensive attempts, the laser guns failed to solve the climate's problem. Each of the many thousands of lasers that we employed worked perfectly and burned large volumes of greenhouse gases. Unfortunately, each consumed volume was immediately replaced with another volume of gases from the gigantic troposphere that surrounds us! Also, after prolonged use, the lasers wore-out, because they were not designed to work for very long periods. So sorry!

I must confess to you that my heart bleeds each time that I must report to you on yet another proposal failing, and I cannot even start to imagine how you feel after each disappointment. Your disappointment is probably multiplied many folds compared to any disappointment that I may feel. Therefore, let us hope that my next report will be a happy one, unlike all my previous ones!!!

Signed: John Roberts, the organization's spokesman.

Operations' Diary of John Roberts
(Top Secret and Private)

02.06.2026

"Dear Diary,

I have reached again the point where I no longer believe that any "Noah's Ark" proposal will work. I am an Economist by profession, and the only scientific knowledge that I had ever acquired was sadly outdated. I acquired it from old Miss Glaser at high school No. 12 in Brookline, and her own scientific knowledge was obtained in the 20th century... However, I constantly use the Internet as a source of scientific knowledge. From my surfing, I learned that although the greenhouse gases are so damaging to the climate, their specific volumes (volume per unit space) are very small, because of their tiny molecular diameters. Therefore, it is not surprising that although we used many thousands of lasers, their narrow, coherent rays missed most of the molecules of the greenhouse gases. However, what is even more distressing is that each burned volume of gases was immediately replenished from the "blanket" of gases that surrounds us.

Scientists, by their nature, must be optimistic and believe that each of their future experiments will work. Otherwise, they would leave their vocations rather quickly and become hermits in some desert... I admire them, but I also pity them since in their fight against the greenhouse gases, alas, they cannot win.

"Noah's Ark" Organization

A non-profit organization, 1300 NW,
Suite 200E, Washington D.C

Announcement No. 9; "Noah's Ark" proposal No. 5: Geo-Engineering of Earth for the removal of the greenhouse gases

(This announcement was written by John
Roberts, the spokesman for "**Noah's Ark**")

05.27.26

"Dear Citizens of the world!

In a few days we shall start with proposal No. 5 that
will be based on "Geo-Engineering" of our earth.
Geo-Engineering is a program intended to improve
a world that God, or Nature, created and adapt it
for Human use. Our scientists examined several
interesting and apparently sensible Geo-Engineering

proposals. However, they were either too difficult to perform, or too dangerous, and were rejected. We were left with one feasible proposal that I shall soon describe. But, before that, I want to describe all the proposals that were suggested to show you that our scientists really tried their best to devise new possibilities.

1. One climatologist suggested to shoot Sulfate particles to the troposphere to mimic the volcanic eruption of the Pilipino Mount Pinatubo in 1991. In that eruption, millions of tons of ash and volcanic debris, as well as Sulfur Dioxide gas, were ejected to the stratosphere. They hid the sun in the vicinity of the eruption and caused a temperature lowering of one to two degrees Centigrade, for several years.

According to that climatologist's suggestion, sulfate aerosols should be sent to the Stratosphere with artillery shells, by aircraft, or inside balloons. These sulfate aerosols will be highly packed frozen sulfide gases such as dimethyl sulfide, Carbonyl Sulfide, hydrogen sulfide, or sulfur dioxide. He said that his proposed method will rapidly take effect, will have very low implementation costs, and that one kilogram of packed gases can offset the effects of several thousand kilograms of Carbon Dioxide. He also added that it should be tried in a small scale in some deserted area, and if found to be environmentally and technologically viable and safe, it should be implemented in a large scale. He said that deliveries of sulfates to the stratosphere could provide a "grace period" of several years until a major reduction in greenhouse gases' production will be implemented by our world government.

All the scientists in the Noah's Ark headquarters liked the "Sulfate idea" and expressed their enthusiasm on hearing it. But one of the organization's advisors, a lawyer who was an expert on climate laws, voiced a strong objection. He said that there are many health hazards and political challenges that are involved in the use of Sulfates, and that Sulfate compounds are known to seriously damage the ozone layer. The volume of Ozone gas in the vicinity of coal burning electrical power plants, that release Sulfates, is always greatly reduced.

The lawyer also added that the Convention on Long-Range Trans-boundary Air Pollution (CLRTAP Convention), compels those countries which had ratified the agreement, to reduce their emissions of all gases, **including sulfates**. Also, starting in 2022, the Montreal Protocol and the Vienna Convention, prohibited the production of all ozone-depleting substances, and Sulfates are the foremost among the listed prohibited substances.

In addition, the lawyer also said that the 2021 amendment to the Clean Air Act gives the United States' Environmental Protection Agency (EPA), the authority to prevent the use of stratospheric Sulfate aerosols. Therefore, the World government, which adopted many of the USA's rulings, will never allow the use of these aerosols.

After a long discussion, Just and Beaufort, with a heavy heart and great reluctance, ruled against the proposal. They consoled the disappointed scientists by promising that if all the other organization's proposals will fail, they will reconsider their decision, and will try to obtain permission from the various authorities to use sulphates. They said that they think that they will be able to get it, even at the cost of a loss of some ozone. Such a loss is damaging, but it is the lesser evil compared to the current climate catastrophe.

2. A few scientists suggested to construct a very large mirror in space made of billions of gold particles. The proposed intended flat mirror will be diagonal to the sun, and thus will reflect part of the sun's rays and heat. True, they said, the mirror proposal is a very expensive one, but should work very well. However, other scientists objected by saying that it will take several years to send enough particles to space to achieve a large mirror, and time is short. Moreover, the mirror

can never be removed, and may cause very low temperatures on earth sometime in the future.

3. One scientist suggested to use an oily liquid that will create a membrane over the surfaces of all oceans and will prevent their evaporation. This suggestion was rejected since the consensus by other scientists was that the strong gales and the high waves of the seas, will certainly shatter the fragile oily membranes.

4. Another proposal that was suggested by a couple of scientists, was "Cloud Seeding". According to this proposal, chemical substances such as silver iodide, potassium iodide or dry ice (solid carbon dioxide) will be dispersed into the Cirrus cloud layer at the height of about 3 miles. These substances will act as crystallization points for the water vapor in the clouds and will cause it to precipitate down as rain. The elimination of the clouds will allow the heat radiated from Earth to escape to outer space. Unfortunately, one scientist, previously from the USA National Research Council (NRC), cited a report which stated that the cloud seeding method was tried by the NRC and does not work. Once again, the proposal was rejected with great regret.

After describing the Geo-Engineering proposals that were rejected, let me describe to you the proposal that was suggested by an old and wise botanist. The purpose of this proposal two-fold: to reduce the concentration of the Carbon Dioxide and water vapor over the oceans and to lower the oceans' temperatures. He said that this proposal is already under study by small scale in several countries, but conclusions of the studies had not been published yet.

The proposal is based on the creation of conditions that will cause a vast growth-enhancement of chlorophyll-containing green algae in all seas. This enhancement will be achieved by the addition of Iron salts, which are an important nutrient for the growth of the green algae, and by also the addition of a supplement of fermented organic material called Compost. Compost is prepared by a process called "Compostation of Manure". Manure is the partial digest of the vegetable fodder that cattle and sheep eat and then excrete. It contains mostly cellulose and lignin. This digest is further fermented by soil bacteria to produce a mixture that is rich in Nitrogenous, phosphoric and potassium molecules. These molecules are essential to all vegetation, including also to algae. As a result of the production of a mass of growth-enhanced algae in the form of a thick carpet, this carpet will float over the surface of all seas and will prevent the heating of the seas by the Sun, thereby preventing the evaporation of seawater into harmful water vapor.

The cooling of the seas will also stop the thawing of glaciers. Also, the green algae, by a process of photosynthesis with their chlorophyll, will transform the Carbon Dioxide in the atmosphere into glucose, which is also essential for algal growth.

All the scientists in the meeting, immediately voiced strong approval of the proposal and it was immediately adopted even without the need for a vote. However, some scientists voiced a stipulation before their final approvement. They wanted to test the idea on one sea to see if the proposal does not have some important snags that might preclude its use. Even the most enthusiastic proponents of the proposal, who wanted to start with the proposal full steam in all seas, finally agreed to adopt this sensible precaution.

The Sea that was chosen as a site for the testing of the efficacy and safety of the proposal, was the Mediterranean Sea, because of the following reasons: the temperature in this sea varies greatly according to its various locations and the time in the year. During July and August, its temperatures are the highest and vary between 18 to 28 degrees centigrade. The part of the sea with the highest summer temperature lies between Cyprus and Israel. One half of this Cyprus-Israel area will be seeded with Iron salts plus compost, and the other half will serve as a control area.

The compost was to be extracted from dairy farms in Cyprus and along the coast of Israel and loaded onto a fleet of large trucks. The trucks will drive to seven seaports along the coasts of Israel and Cyprus. There the mushy compost will be pumped from the trucks into the holds of well-scrubbed oil tankers and solutions of Iron salts will be added to the compost. Then the suspensions of compost plus Iron salts will be spread, again with the use of pumps, over the surface of the experimental half of the sea.

The Mediterranean Sea abounds with large quantities of thousands of types of fish, and with hundred seafood species: crabs, crayfish, prawn, lobsters, and shrimp as well as cockle, cuttlefish, mussels, octopi, and oysters. Therefore, it is very important to determine whether the new algal proposal will affect the existence of the various species that are harvested from the sea. It should be remembered that with the failing of agriculture all over the World, fish and seafood creatures now serve as a very important source of food. In addition to the determination of a possible loss of species and a decrease in harvesting, two more parameters will be measured in the control area and in the "composted" one:

1. Can the floating algal carpet reduce the temperature of the sea beneath it as expected? Accurate thermometers that will continually record

the temperatures throughout several days, will be sunk into various depths below the surface in both experimental and control areas

2. Fisherman will harvest the fish and seafood organisms from the "Composted" and the control sparse areas and will bring them ashore for comparative weighing. Marine biologists will examine the harvest for a possible loss of species in the "Composted" area. Our scientists are very hopeful that this proposal will decrease the sea temperatures and will not affect too excessively the harvested quantities and species of fish and seafood organisms.

Signed: John Roberts, the organization's spokesman

"Noah's Ark" Organization
non-profit organization, 1300 NW,
Suite 200E, Washington D.C

Announcement No. 10: Noah Ark's proposal No. 5: Postponement of the Geo-Engineering of Earth for the removal of the greenhouse gases

(This announcement was written by John
Roberts, the spokesman for "**Noah's Ark**")

09.30.2026

"Dear Citizens of the world!

Owing to the need to inform you of the outcome of all "Noah's Ark" proposals, we, very regretfully, must inform you the proposal No. 5 is now suspended for some unknown time, although it may be revived at some later time. I must admit that in my hopeful dreams I saw myself, finally, declaring victory.

True, the proposal exceeded the expectations of all our scientists with regards to the sea temperature under the Green Algal blanket and the concentration of the Greenhouse gases over the algal blanket: the temperatures at sea level and below sea level were reduced by 1.5 to 4 degrees Centigrade, depending on the depths measured. Moreover, the concentration of both water vapor and Carbon Dioxide over the sea level were considerably reduced. However, unfortunately, the damage to all types of fish and seafood organisms was large. Their numbers declined considerably and since harvests from the seas currently supply about 20-25% of the World's food requirements, the proposal was suspended temporarily, at least, for the present.

Signed: John Roberts, the organization's spokesman.

Operations' Diary of John Roberts
(Top Secret and Private)

10.15.2026

"Dear Diary,

I must admit that my confidence in the proposals of the organization is now somewhat on the upswing, despite the present suspension of proposal 5. Who knows, perhaps there is still hope for the future?

BOOK 2

MATTER AND ANTI-MATTER

CHAPTER 3

The Ad-Hoc Emergency proposal No. 7

efore the issuing of the announcement on the initiation of "Noah's Ark" proposal No. 6, a discussion was held on Skype between Just and Beaufort. The two chairmen often talked to solve current problems and the following is a transcript of that discussion:

Just: "Hi, Walter, my dear friend, what is going on at your end? Did, Mary give birth yet? A few days had already passed since you told me that it would soon happen?"

Beaufort: "Hi there, Bill my friend. Yes, I have a new grandson called Bernard Jr. after his father! He weighed 7 pounds at birth, and his crying voice can compete now with that of the best coloratura soprano from the Metropolitan ... He made me even happier than I was when I acquired my first company!"

Just: "Wonderful, Bill! Wonderful! Good luck! Please

congratulate Mary and Bernard on my behalf! And now, let us discuss another matter altogether: Some time ago we have decided that if we fail with proposals No.1 to No. 5, we shall start with proposal 6. But, as both of us know, a successful outcome of proposal 6 is somewhat doubtful … Therefore, we have decided, both of us simultaneously, to devise a new proposal, "Noah's Ark" emergency proposal No. 7."

<u>Beaufort</u>: "True! Indeed we did. This coincidence is amazing. I must say that it is a case where two geniuses think alike …"

<u>Just</u>: "Well then, if you agree, let us issue, before the next announcement on proposal No. 6, an announcement on proposal No. 7. It will say that proposal No. 7 will be activated only if we fail with proposal No. 6 and that it is a large extension of our previous welfare proposal. We shall say that almost all our remaining wealth, which is still considerable, will be transferred to the combined financial fund of our volunteer tycoons. Proposal No. 7 shall offer immediate help by air to all the climate's refugees, using robust transport planed. This way, if we fail in our ambitious proposal No. 6, we shall provide immediate worldly relief with proposal No. 7..."

Just nodded agreement, and after farewell words, the connection was terminated. Two days later, announcement No. 11 on emergency proposal No.7 came out.

"Noah's Ark" Organization
A non-profit organization, 1300 NW,
Suite 200E, Washington D.C

Announcement No. 11; "Noah's Ark" proposal No. 7: An emergency ad-hoc proposal for refugees, that will dramatically extend our previous help organization

(This announcement was written by Bill just and Walt Beaufort, Co-Chairmen of "Noah's Ark")

01.11.27

"Dear Citizens of the world!

Please note: If proposal No. 6 that will soon start, will fail, we shall activate emergency proposal no. 7. This is a proposal that will continues the welfare enterprise that our volunteer tycoons took over from us at our request. However, it is to be extended many folds since Beaufort and I shall return to it with all our remaining money and resources. This proposal will supply, by robust cargo planes such as super Hercules, food, Medicare, and medical supplies. These planes can withstand the weather onslaughts. At present, the number of such planes in the World is not large enough, and therefore we shall immediately commission the production of many new like these planes. In addition to existence staples they will also transfer refugees to well- equipped camps on high lands. However, we still hope that proposal No. 7 may not be required, since **proposal 6 – our best proposal, will soon start!!!**

Signed: Walt Beaufort and Bill Just

Operations' Diary of John Roberts
(Top Secret and Private)

02.15.2027

Dear Diary,

Finally, after a very long period of disappointment, I hope that proposal No. 7, announced by my two bosses, will, finally, put our organization on the right track! It is a proposal with a lot of meat on its bones … True, it is just an emergency proposal intended to answer a possible failure of proposal No. 6. However, perhaps our climate will finally have pity us, during the term of the implementation of proposal5 and return to a normal mode.

I hope that proposal No. 6 will succeed as promised. If not, God forbid, at least with proposal No. 7 in effect, at least I shall not have to load mournful submission of one failure after another with a strong buffeting to my psyche.

I am not qualified to grade proposal No. 6, that will soon start: "the production of **Anti-Matter** energy and its harnessing it into cluster bomblets." Please God that our scientists, who swear by this proposal, are finally right.

CHAPTER 4

Choosing a site for proposal No. 6

"Noah's Ark" Organization
A non-profit organization, 1300 NW,
Suite 200E, Washington D.C.

Announcement No. 12: Choosing of a suitable site for Noah's Ark's" proposal No. 6.

(A note from John Robert's: This announcement was written by Gennady Samoikhin, a Ukrainian speleologist (an expert cave climber), (with a suitable translation from Russian by a Noah's Ark's translators)

02.12.27

"Dear Citizens of the world!

Several weeks ago, I was approached by two scientific advisers from the "Noah's Ark" organization. Since they learned that I have studied all the important caves in the globe, they asked me to recommend to them a cave that will fit two major requirements: A. That it will be very deep, and B. that it will be as far as possible from any human settlement. I was told that the organization proposes to develop an extremely powerful explosive of a sort never seen before, and that in case of an accidental mishap, God forbid, the cave should be in an area completely free of any residents.

I did not hesitate even for a moment and named the Krubera-Voronja cave in Abkhazia. Abkhazia is a small country on the eastern coast of the Black Sea and the south-western flank of the Caucasus Mountains. It is in the South of Russia and north-westly to Georgia. Abkhazia has a population of around 240,000 people and its capital is called Sukhumi. Abkhazia severed itself from Georgia and was recognized only by Russia and a small number of other countries.

Aside from the capital city of Sukhumi, Abkhazia has two medium sized cities called Gagra and Sochi. Sochi is a famous resort city which hosts conventions, and that Putin visits for vacation. It has a good airport which will facilitate the transfer of all materials required for the "Noah's Ark" enterprise. Railroad tracks and roads can be paved from Sochi to the caves, but will require a lot of work, since the land is craggy and rocky. However, at least, the distance from Sochi to the caves is relatively short.

Krubera-Voronja (or just 'Krubera', as it is often called) is a very large and deep cave that is the deepest ever found to-date. In addition to its depth, it also has an added advantage. There is a second, much wider and bigger cave that is attached to it that is called Kyubishevskaya. This second cave is not as deep as the Krubera cave but contains huge halls and galleries that are a lot bigger than those of Krubera's.

The Krubera cave was first explored down to a short depth by a group of Ukrainian speleologists who named it in honor of Alexander Kruber, a famous Ukrainian speleologist. Next came speleologists from many countries who mapped the cave all the way down to a depth of 2080 meters. The Kyubishevskia cave was named after a Russian woman-speleologist called Elena Kyubisheva who fell to her death while exploring the cave.

Both caves are in a group of connecting mountain ranges called Arabica, that is part of the Caucasus mountains. The Arabica ranges are made of Karstic rocks that were formed by the dissolution and fusion of limestone and dolomite in geological times. Dolomite is a widespread mineral made of Calcium and Magnesium Carbonates. In general, Karstic rocks are soft and easily drilled and contain many caves and streams that provide large supplies of water.

At the end of this announcement there is a map of Abkhazia and its neighboring countries. A second chart below this map, shows a vertical cross-sectional cut of the two connected caves together.

The people of the "Noah's Ark" organization also asked me to recommend a suitable site for a Cyclotron which should be placed within a long circular tunnel that they proposal to drill. The Cyclotron will produce their new explosive. I suggested that the Krubera cave may be best suited for this purpose. They also needed to prepare a large workers' camp that would be far away from the Cyclotron, and I suggested a very large gallery in the kyubishevskaya cave.

As can be seen in the vertical cross-sectional cut of the two caves, they contain vertical, horizontal, and oblique tunnels. I suggested that movement of persons and transport of heavy equipment in the vertical tunnels, can be achieved by building suitable elevators. Movement and transport in the horizontal and oblique tunnels can be achieved using escalators. Where the tunnels are not smooth, they can be easily carved and scraped since the Karstic walls are relatively soft.

There is an accepted misconception that the air of caves is suffocating, beset with toxic gases and is also inflammable. This is true for mines, but not for caves! On the contrary, caves have cracks in the rocks and have several small openings through which air easily flows. Moreover, the high humidity in the caves precipitates all damaging dust particles. Since there is not any vegetation in the caves and, therefore, no allergens, some caves in the world even serve as havens for the treatment of pulmonary patients. There are no zoological species in both caves, aside from a few species of blind salamanders and worms.

In summary, the two caves perfectly conform to all Noah's Ark's specifications. Finally, I wish great success to all Noah's Ark employees who are going to spend time in the caves to fashion a weapon which will fight the greenhouse gases!

Signed: Gennady Samoikhin, speleologist

A map of Abkhazia and its neighboring countries

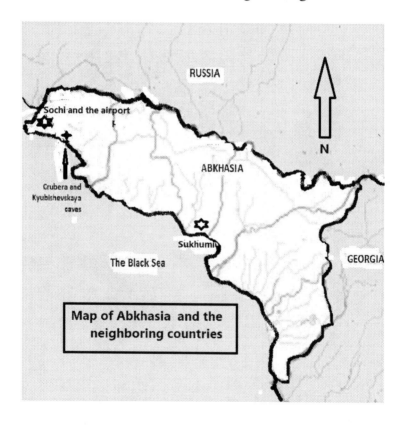

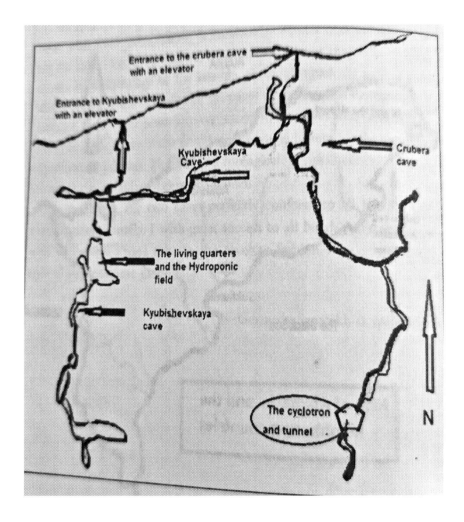

Chapter 5

"Noah's Ark" proposal No. 6 goes on track

"And God said unto Noah, the end of all flesh is come before me; for the earth is filled with violence through them; and, behold, I will destroy them with the earth. Make thee an ark of gopher wood; rooms shalt thou make in the ark, and shalt pitch it within and without with pitch. And this is the fashion which thou shalt make it of: The length of the ark shall be three hundred cubits, the breadth of it fifty cubits, and the height of it thirty cubits A window shalt thou make to the ark, and in a cubit shalt thou finish it above; and the door of the ark shalt thou set in the side thereof; with lower, second, and third stories shalt thou make it."

The Old Testament; Genesis; chapter 6

After the collapse of proposals No. 1 to No. 5, Just and Beaufort activated "Noah's Ark" proposal No. 6. For that purpose, they and their advisers started to recruit specialists from various areas that would be required for the most optimal performance of the proposal. Proposal No. 6 is going to be both more extensive than the previous ones and would also require considerably more time to complete. Just and Beaufort, at the advice of their human resources manager, Mrs. Iris Schwabé, decided to use the method of defined workgroups, like the "work brigades" employed by the Russians and the Chinese when they planned to undertake very large building or cultural enterprises. She said that this approach would lead to effective, well-coordinated and simultaneous work on several sub-projects, and would lead to a considerable timesaving.

Iris Schwabé, which was borrowed from one of Beaufort's companies because of her proficiency in "head-hunting" of managers, immediately started a search for leaders of the work groups. As soon as that task was completed, a new announcement of the organization was issued for the hiring of professional workers for proposal No. 6.

"Noah's Ark" Organization
A non-profit organization, 1300 NW,
Suite 200E, Washington D.C

Announcement No. 13; "Noah's Ark's" proposal
No. 6: The use of Anti-Matter cluster bomblets
for the removal of the greenhouse gases

(This announcement was written by Iris
Schwabé, the human resources manager
for "Noah's Ark" organization)

04.18.27

"Dear Citizens of the world!

My name is Iris Schwabé, and I am the human
resources manager in charge of hiring personnel for
Noah's Ark's proposal No. 6. We need to hire about
400 professional workers with the kinds of expertise
that I shall enumerate below. Qualified workers, men,

and women alike, who wish to join, will undergo a strict selection by the supervisors of the six workgroups that we have established. Suitable professional applicants will also have to pass a physical checkup and psychological tests to determine their ability to work with other people of various nationalities.

The present announcement will list the description of the specific jobs required for each workgroup. All the workers who will be hired, will receive excellent salaries that would be fourfold higher than the average current international salary of the countries of Western Europe. Those who are presently unemployed, due to the current economic situation, will also receive this quadruple calculated salary. All The workers will also receive generous work benefits and health- and retirement- and insurance proposals that will be described to them when they are hired.

Moreover, all mortgage payments that the workers currently have, as well as their insurance and health premiums, will be paid by our organization during their two-year stint on the job. The organization will also continue to pay the premiums for any retirement proposal that the workers have if they will lose their current jobs because of their long absence from their previous jobs. As you can see, we are doing all we can to attract expert workers.

The work in proposal No. 6 of the "**Noah's Ark** consortium is important for the whole world and will be carried out within two large caves under the highest safety standards. It is recommended that you read all of announcement No.13 and its maps information on the location and nature of the caves that will be used in proposal No. 6.

We realize that it will be difficult for most of you to leave your families for the 2-year period of the work. Therefore, we have decided to allow you to bring your families with you. Note however, that due to the shortage of housing in the camp, only your first-degree relatives – wives, sweethearts, husbands, and children, can come with you. Also, no pets that your children might have will be allowed to come. Your elderly dependents, such as fathers, mothers, aunts, and uncles, who required your support before your enrollment, will be placed in very good retirement homes. If they prefer to stay in their homes, they will receive caretakers and all other types of support. In addition, we shall supply computers to any elderly dependents who do not have them, and shall teach them how to use Skype, so that they will be able to communicate with you and see you from afar.

Following is a brief description of the main jobs that will be performed in the two caves, according to their priority schedule:

1. The organization will pave a wide road and will build railroad tracks from the Sochi airport to the caves, 60 miles. This is going to be a difficult job, that will require a lot of scraping and drilling and the use of explosives to dig a straight course in the craggy and rocky Arabica range.

   Any jagged walls in the tunnels, galleries, and halls of the two caves will also be scraped, drilled, and smoothed and will be overlaid with ultra-strong composite plastic sheets.

2. A large housing camp for all the workers will be built inside a cave called Kyubishevskaya, because of the following three reasons:

A. The workers will need to live inside the cave, so that they will be shielded from any mishap that may occur during the production of the new Anti-Matter explosive that we propose to produce in the second, distant, Krubera cave.

B. The ground round near the caves is extremely uninhabitable due to very harsh climatic conditions on the range inside which the caves reside – it is exposed to very strong and cold winds blowing from the South-west of the Black Sea.

C. Proposal 6 must be performed very urgently before our Earth is lost, and we don't want to waste time on the transportation of the workers from houses in Sochi or in other habitable areas. The camp inside the Kyubishevskaya cave will contain prefabricated wooden huts which will be produced in Russia, and which will contain all the facilities that normal apartments have. The camp will be run like an apartment hotel and will have all the facilities that any small city might have.

The bomblets will be exploded in the troposphere to destroy the blanket of the greenhouse gases that surrounds our earth. **Anti-Matter** is a new and extremely powerful form of energy that had never existed before. What exactly it is, and how it will work, will be described below.

A large area inside the Kyubishevskaya workers' camp will be dedicated to hydroponic agriculture intended for the purpose of eliminating the costly transport of fresh vegetables and fruit from Abkhazia or from Russia. The camp will also contain fishponds and a few cows for fresh milk for babies. The cows will be fed with hydroponically grown fodder. Expert mineworkers will drill and scrape the Karstic walls which are relatively soft, to supply big enough galleries for the hydroponic garden, the fishponds and the cow shed.

The tunnels, halls, and galleries will be coated with ultra-strong composite plastic sheets. The Arabica ranges are relatively high, about 3500 meters above the Black Sea level, and normally completely devoid of rains. But, because of the current rough climate conditions, the caves are now visited by strong torrents of winds, and, therefore, the two caves will be locked with strong convex Perspex covers that will be opened and closed electrically.

Please note that all the services in the camp such as the catering, the teaching the of children and medical and recreational services will be free. Teaching will be performed in a kindergarten, an elementary School, and a High-School that will have modern teaching aids, books, computers and will be served by qualified teachers. The camp will have a coffee-house and a dining-hall, where the food will be prepared by professional cooks. The camp will also have a theater hall for the projection of movies, for meeting of all the workers, and for amateur theatrical groups if such will be present among you. The theater will also serve for religious worship that will be conducted by clerics of the three major religions. The clerics will take turns according to a pre-arranged schedule.

The camp will also have sports facilities such as lighted Tennis courts, and soccer and Basketball courts. A pub in the camp will have a karaoke machine, Jukeboxes and will serve beer and other alcoholic drinks. All the facilities will stay open at all hours, since the work in the project will be carried out continuously, with three 8-hour shifts and on weekends, because of the pressing need to fight the climate.

A few years ago, a camp for 10,000 pyramid workers was uncovered in Giza, Egypt, at about 1000 feet from the Sphinx. Near the camp were fences for cattle and sheep that were brought each day from the fertile areas of the Nile. The site also contained slaughterhouses and kitchens for the roasting and cooking of meat. The engineers and various experts were fed with beef, which was a delicacy, while the simple workers were fed mutton which was cheaper. Such class distinctions as those that existed Giza will not occur in our project! All of you, whether you are a professor, or a cleaning lady will have the same benefits and privileges!

Following below, find the names of the six managers of the various workgroups, the types of experts and workers needed for each group, and the E-mails of the managers. If you wish to join our enterprise, send your résumé, a list of jobs that you have held, the number of dependents that you wish to bring with you, and their ages. List also all your current work-benefits, payments, and mortgages that you want us to continue paying.

Note that you must be able to speak (but not necessarily to read and write) **one** of the following languages that will be used in the project: English, French, German and Russian. If your future manager does not speak your language, your résumé will be translated for him. Simultaneous interpreters of all the four official languages listed will function in shifts, both in the caves and with the managers in the hiring interviews. We shall transport suitable professionals to the caves from their homes, free of charge. However, do not resign your present jobs, but ask your bosses for 2-4 weeks leave of absence for your interviews and testing. This way you will not lose your jobs in case of a rejection of your applications. We shall not be responsible of any loss of lobs.

List of the managers of the 6 workgroups, their e-mail addresses, and the kinds of professionals that the require:

1. **Anatoli Shevchenko**, Civil Engineer. He needs workers for. building and transport. Various drivers). The professionals are listed below. His mail is <u>antsh@Noah.com.</u>

    *   Various types of masons and builders
    *   Carpenters
    *   Electricians
    *   Plumbers
    *   Road and railroad builders

- Truck drivers
- Train drivers
- Steel construction experts and metal workers
- Plasterers
- Air conditioning and ventilation experts.

2. **John Britten**, Mining and Safety Engineer, drilling of cave-galleries and tunnels, jobr@noah. com He requires:

- Miners
- Stonecutters
- Cellphone- and online- Communication experts
- Controlled Explosion experts
- Operators of Electric generator
- Electricians
- Elevator- and escalator- designers and operators
- Bulldozer- and excavator- operators.

3. **Professor Francine Dumas,** Orthopedic surgeon, Director of the camp's Hospital and its Research Institute, Medical treatment of accidents and of rare contagious diseases that might exist in the caves, the excavations, and the caves' water springs. fd@Noah.com.

She requires:

- Analytical laboratory technicians, Physicians, nurses, and Pharmacists.

- Imaging experts
- Microbiologists
- Prosthesis builders
- Molecular geneticists.

4. **Franz Obermeyer**, Hotel manager and former chef, in charge of the operation of the dining hall, the schools, the workers' huts, the sports, and the entertainment facilities. fro@noah.com. He requires:

- Kindergarten, elementary school, and high school teachers
- Cooks
- Librarians and information specialists
- Quadri-lingual Translators (English, French, German and Russian)
- Tailors
- Laundry operators
- Athletics-, Swimming-, Tennis-, dancing-, Yoga And Tai-chi instructors
- Hydroponics experts
- A dairy farmer
- A Seeds' custodian for the hydroponic fields.

5. **Professor Li-Hua Chen**, Physics Professor, Nobel prize winner of the year 2021 in physics of sub-atomic particles lhc@Noah.com. She requires:

- Climatologists

- Highly skilled computer programmers and operators of Cray Supercomputers
- Machinists and operators of computerized lathes
- Developers and operators of high-output Electromagnets
- Deep freeze operators
- Electronic engineers
- Physicists with experience in the operation of cyclotrons from research institutes, with a preference for Cern veterans.

6. **Professor Tom Evans**, Professor of Psychology, and Polygraph technology, <u>te@Noah.com.</u>

He requires:

- Clinical Psychologists and Polygraph operators
- Human resources experts
- Religious leaders: a Minister, a priest, a Rabbi, and a Mullah (Muslim preacher).

Mrs. Schwabe then added to the proposal:

Following is important information that Professor Evans asked me to deliver to all the applicants who were found to be suitable professionally. He dictated the notice to me, and I transfer it to you verbatim:

"Dear Applicants:

All applicants who were found to be professionally suitable by the managers of the work groups, will undergo medical testing which will be performed by a team headed by Professor Dumas. Next, they will be tested by me and by my staff with various psychological questionnaires, also including a Polygraph test. This testing will determine if, together with a healthy body, you are also psychologically "robust." Those who will fail our psychological tests are certainly sane enough, but we believe that they will not be able to withstand the harsh conditions of the long stay in the caves. All the applicants who will not be suitable, will be transported home and will be generously compensated for the workdays lost because of the selection and testing.

In addition, if you are accepted, I, as the manager in charge of your morale and psychological well-being, can supply you with mild tranquilizing drugs for a short time until you get acclimatized. This is because you are going to live under the most unusual conditions, similar only, perhaps, to those of submarine-personnel or Antarctic scientists. Therefore, don't be ashamed to ask for the tranquillizers.

Also, I'll try to ensure that your sexual needs are fulfilled, because they are important for your psychological well-being. Many of you may be married or in liaisons, and I recommend that you should bring your spouses or sweethearts with you. However, for those men and women among you who are not attached or married, I shall try to act as a "matchmaker", if they will not find suitable companions among their single fellow-workers. For that purpose, I shall open a confidential site in our intranet, called <u>Matchmaker@Noah.com,</u> which you may use. Even married people may use this service, since I realize that under the imminent fear of death by the climate, peoples' mores have changed.

Our pub, "The happy cave", will also serve as a useful 'Cupid'. The hospital will supply birth control means to those who may want them. Our organization will not prevent any couples from giving birth during their 2-year service in the project and will supply the newborns with the best medical and nutritional care. However, since space in the camp is limited, we do not encourage procreation. Also, crying babies may interfere with the sleep of your neighbors, who may need to work in a job that requires their utmost concentration. Finally, I would like to mention that the caves will be well-lit 24/7 since light is very important for a psychological well-being.

Finally, I would like to welcome all who would join our ranks and I wish all of you success in your work in the caves, your work is so very vital to the survival of all humanity."

Here Mrs. Schwabé took again the writing license: in "Noah's Ark" proposal No. 6 we shall produce **Anti-Matter** and will pack it in cluster bomblets (grenades). These bomblets will be exploded at various heights of the troposphere to get rid of the greenhouse gases. Although I always loved physics and studied it in high-school, I am not qualified to explain what **Anti-Matter** is, and how it will work. Therefore, I asked our chief Physicist, Professor Li-Hua Chen, a Nobel prize winner in sub-atomic particles, to write for you an explanation of this extremely powerful force of nature for you. Here is what she wrote:

"Hello everybody.

The Universe around us is made of **Matter** – atoms and molecules of many elements (104 by the last count, but some of them were artificially made in small quantities). This **Matter** that surrounds us is the only material that all things are made of (and certainly not of "Sugar and spice and everything nice"...). But, about a hundred years ago, a new kind of material was discovered that was much later called **Anti-Matter.** Its existence was first inferred when a scientist by the name of Dirac formulated a theory accompanied by equations that described the movement of electrons in electrical and magnetic fields. One of the unexpected outcomes of his equations, suggested the existence of a new type of sub-atomic particle which was not recognized previously: an **Anti-Electron.**

Dirac's equations predicted that for each "Normal" **negatively** charged electron of **Matter,** there should be an opposing twin electron of the same properties but that carries an opposite, **positive** electrical charge –that is, an **Anti-Matter electron.** Such positively charged **Anti-Matter electrons** were eventually called **positrons.** Whole atoms that contain positrons are **Anti-Matter atoms.** The existence of the previously presumed **Anti-Matter electrons** and **atoms** was later confirmed by many studies.

Anti-Matter positrons and atoms are absent from most parts of the universe, including our world. Scientists believe that a few fractions of a second after the "Big Bang" that created the Cosmos, there was an equal number of **Matter** and **Anti-Matter** electrons and atoms. But, because of some unknown mechanism, **Anti-Matter electrons** and **Anti-Matter atoms** disappeared. However, **Anti-Matter** does exist for a very short time when **Normal-Matter whole stars** are sucked into **black holes** or **neutron stars.** When this happens, the stars completely disintegrate. This destructive event spews out a tremendous amount of Gamma and x-ray radiation and an unbelievable number of **Anti-Matter** positive electrons (**positrons**) per second. Now, when **Anti-Matter** meets **Normal**

Matter, both are annihilated. Free **Anti-Matter** does not exist in our world, and it needs to be artificially manufactured.

I do not intend to make astrophysicists (those who study the cosmos) of you. Therefore, I shall not explain what black holes and Neutron stars are. Suffice it to say that we shall produce **Anti-Matter** in a cyclotron that will be in the uninhabited Krubera cave and shall pack it into special cluster bomblets (grenades). The produced **anti-matter** will not be allowed to explode - it will stay in the center of the bomblets away from their **Normal Matter** casings. The cluster bomblets will be flown to the troposphere where they will be exploded when their casings will burst open by a signal from the ground. Such enormous explosions will destroy the **Normal-Matter greenhouse gases**

Anti-Matter is artificially manufactured. It is produced in extremely complicated machines called Cyclotrons. Cyclotrons are to be found in the European sub-particle research center called Cern and in quite a few other centers in the world. The Cyclotron is a cyclic particle-accelerator that accelerates charged atoms and sub-atomic particles to high energies and speed in very long circular tunnels and produces Anti-particles.

These artificially made **Anti Matter** particles are obtained by repeated passage through a magnetic field produced in the tunnels of the cyclotron by the use of huge electromagnets. During this process, the accelerated **Normal Matter** particles lose electrons and become **Anti-Matter** particles.

In the inhabitant-free Krubera cave, we shall build an accelerating cyclotron but that will not require a 27 kilometers-long tunnel as in CERN. Due to a revolutionary invention of mine that I shall not publicize here, our tunnel will be only 2 miles long. At the end of its path there will be a companion Decelerating (braking) Cyclotron, that will operate in Vacuum and will freeze down the anti-mater produced in the Accelerating Cyclotron. Under very strict safety conditions, my physicists will pack the frozen Anti-Matter into the special cluster bomblets that I mentioned above.

My technic to produce Anti-Matter works perfectly well. However, the method of the suspension of the Anti-Matter in the center of the bomblets to prevent them from annihilation through the touching of the Normal Matter casing of the bomblets, has not been solved yet. This problem will be tackled by the experts that I have enlisted. I know that I have "fed" you now with incomprehensible scientific information. Still, what is important for me to stress to you is that believe that we shall succeed in fashioning an excellent weapon against the greenhouse gases."

Here Iris added final remarks to the announcement: "A note to those who will join our project: in all your work-shifts, the men, and women alike, should wear work clothes consisting of padded trousers and shirts to overcome the low, but still reasonable temperature in the caves. The uniforms will have different colors (six colors - in accordance with the six workgroups of the project). These colors will help in your identification. In addition, you will wear identification tags with your name and expertise. Moreover, we shall supply you with walkie-talkie instruments like the ones that policemen carry. Each workgroup will have its own frequency channel.

Finally, I want to wish all of those who will be part of our proposal 6, and also the whole world, great success in our enterprise.

Signed: Iris Schwabé, human resources manager

Operations' Diary of John Roberts
(Top Secret and Private)

Date: 03.01.2027

Dear Diary,

I did not participate in the writing of the last three last announcements of "Noah's Ark" (Numbers 11, 12 and 13). They were written by Bill Just and Walt Beaufort themselves, the speleologist Samoikhin and my good friend Iris Schwabé. Therefore, I had enough time to examine several aspects of proposal No. 6, including those that were not published in the above-mentioned announcements.

I must admit that I am exceedingly impressed by the meticulous preparation and the obvious perfection that went into Proposal 6. I was also told that when the destroying of the greenhouse gases will occur, it is planned that a sufficient volume of gases will be left for an accurate regulation of the air temperature.

Despite the hope expressed above, to allay some misgivings that I still harbored with regards of the proposal, I spoke by Skype with Professor Li-Hua. She was already in Krubera to oversee the instalment of the Cyclotron, its infrastructure and the digging of its acceleration and deceleration tunnels. I asked her to "level with me", and to tell me what really the chances for a successful culmination of the proposal are. She answered me that the production of Anti-Matter will succeed very well. However, she admitted that the packaging question is still unsolved, and still requires a lot of research. However, she claimed that she had hired excellent physicists to work on the problem and believes that it can be solved. I jokingly answered that perhaps she ought to hire a few supermarket's packing assistants to help her … Yet, the possession of the information that I "fished" from her, made me worry in earnest about the fate of my family and that of the world's.

CHAPTER 6

First successes

About 18 months had passed since the start of the first of "Noah's Ark" proposals. During this period, five of the proposals had already failed. But then, six months after the start of proposal No. 6, it finally started to bear first fruits. John Roberts published, every month or two, announcements that brought some hope to the hearts of all the citizens of the world. They came at the time when they barely managed to cope with the continuous worsening of the climate.

- Announcement number 14 reported on the completion of the road and railway lines from Sochi to both Abkhazian caves.
- Announcement number 15 told that the walls of all the tunnels, galleries, and halls in the caves were scraped,

drilled, and smoothed, and were overlaid with ultra-strong composite plastic sheets.

- Announcement number 16 reported on the completion of the construction of a large transportation network of vertical, horizontal, and diagonal elevators and escalators.

- Announcement number 17 informed to the world that the workers' camp with all its auxiliary service buildings is now ready to receive the professional workers who were selected. A skeleton crew in the caves already worked feverishly to start the operation of all the services and teaching facilities. The rest of the workers and their families were notified when and where they would be picked up and transported to the caves.

- Announcement number 18 told the world that the 2-mile-long Cyclotron tunnels had been dug and contained along their length rooms for the installation of the huge electro-magnets, the computers, and the supercooling equipment. It also reported on the arrival of the skilled physicists for the operation of the accelerating and decelerating cyclotrons, and of programmers for the superfast Cray computers.

Then to top it all, came announcement No. 19:

"Noah's Ark" Organization
A non-profit organization, 1300 NW,
Suite 200E, Washington D.C

Announcement No. 19; "Noah's Ark's" proposal No. 6: The use of Anti-Matter cluster bomblets for the removal of the greenhouse gases.

This announcement was written by John Roberts,
the spokesman for "Noah's Ark" organization)

01.15.2028

Dear Citizens of the world!

We are happy to announce that both the accelerating Cyclotron and the supercooled-decelerating cyclotron have arrived in the Krubera cave. They were built according to Professor Li-Hua's specifications by one of the most advanced Cyclotron-construction companies. They are already installed in place and underwent several trial runs. Even before the arrival of the cyclotrons, all the 410 qualified workers and their families have already arrived and found their wooden huts and the camp's facilities ready for them.

However, concurrently with all the joy of our continuing success, I have the sad duty of informing you that one of our most devoted workers, Frank Hopper, a miner who specialized in controlled explosions, died. His job was to blow sticking bumps in the elevator shafts of the caves. He drilled a hole in such a bump for the placing of an explosive, but this hole exposed a hidden spring of boiling water that flooded him, and he suffered third-degree burns. Despite all the efforts of our experienced medical team, he passed away. All that remained for the organization to do is to take care of his family. We shall accompany them throughout life. May he rest in peace!

Signed: John Roberts, the organization's spokesman

CHAPTER 7

Happy Tiding

Many newspapermen parked near the houses of the relatives of many workers to obtain inside information and human-interest stories from the project. The families of the project workers in the caves, who were connected by Skype and Internet to the outside world, also did their share to pass information to various newspapers. The communication from inside the caves was blocked by its walls. However, the project's communication engineers, and steel workers built a high antenna made of steel rods and links that could withstand the winds that blew very forcefully on the Arabica range. This antenna and a fiber optic cable allowed all communication traffic to the world, and back from it to get through.

"Noah's Ark" Organization

A non-profit organization, 1300 NW,
Suite 200E, Washington D.C

Announcement No. 20; "Noah's Ark's" proposal No. 6: The use of Anti-Matter cluster bomblets for the removal of the greenhouse gases

This announcement was written by John Roberts,
the spokesman for "Noah's Ark" organization

03.21.2028

Dear Citizens of the world,

We are happy to announce that one of the two most vital projects of proposal No. 6 – the production of Anti-Matter – is now ready to start. This memorable event was officially celebrated in a party in which Just and Beaufort, who permanently reside now in the caves, congratulated all workers. Within a few days after the party, the physicists already produced several grams of Anti-Matter. But, as we have described in earlier announcements, **Anti-Matter** cannot be stored in containers made of **Normal Matter,** because it will react with the walls of the containers leading to immediate annihilation. Small amounts of Anti-Matter can be contained by a combination of electric and magnetic fields in a device called a Pennington trap. Alternatively, Anti-Matter particles can be supercooled and trapped using a magneto-optical or magnetic trap. However, the two storing devices described here, are too cumbersome and are not suitable for mass production and shooting into the troposphere in large numbers. Therefore, the solution of the Anti-Matter packing into bomblets still awaits solution.

Signed: John Roberts, the organization's spokesman

CHAPTER 8

A terrible disaster

Three weeks had passed since the publishing of the optimistic announcement No. 21, and the whole world eagerly waited for additional happy announcements, but these failed to appear. The usual E-mails or Skype chats from the cave team and their families to the outside also stopped abruptly, without any explanation. This lack of communication from the caves caused a lot of worry worldwide, because of fear that something tragic happened to the project.

Communication experts who were questioned by various newspapermen and the relatives of the workers said that, most probably, the communication antenna near the caves had collapsed because of the terrible winds on the Arabica range. However, on the fourth week of silence from the caves, a terrible announcement was published from Noah's ark headquarters:

"Noah's Ark" Organization
A non-profit organization, 1300 NW,
Suite 200E, Washington D.C

Announcement No. 22; "Noah's Ark's" proposal
No. 6: The use of Anti-Matter cluster bomblets
for the removal of the greenhouse gases

This announcement was written in deep
grief by John Roberts, the spokesman
for "Noah's Ark" organization)

02.18.2028

Dear Citizens of the world,

Like all of you we worried about the fate of "Noah's
Ark's" team and their families in the last 3 weeks and
we hoped that the loss of communication with the
caves was temporary. However, to our deep grief, we
must notify you that the project had been destroyed

and all its people died by an immense explosion that was caused by the Anti-Matter that was being manufactured in the Krubera cave.

Several days ago, we sent a helicopter to find out what happened to the project. The pilot could not reach the site because of the terrible winter winds on the Arabica range, and was hurled down to earth after five miles of flight. He was lucky to escape from the helicopter's wreck and had to walk back to the Sochi Airport. This five-mile walk took a whole day, because he had to hide behind some boulders on the way and could move only during short lulls of winds.

On coming back to Sochi, he called us and said that when he reached a maximum height in his flight before crashing, he scanned the site with binoculars and did not see any communication antenna. He recommended that we hire very large bulldozers or heavy battle tanks from the Russians, or the Abkhazians, to reach the caves and determine whether only the antenna collapsed or whether the caves themselves were also destroyed.

We followed his suggestion and the Russian government sent to the caves three heavy battle tanks that remained from the war period, with teams of engineers and paramedics. Unfortunately, the teams drove back to Sochi with the worst of news! The Perspex coverings over the entrances to the two caves were completely shattered, and they could not explore the caves because the entrance-tunnels were blocked with rocks and sand. They inserted a metal pole carrying a walkie-talkie into blocking pile of rocks and sand down to a depth of sixty feet and did not receive any call for help ... The two teams waited for four more days at the site hoping that any residents in the caves will drill through the wreckage but to no avail.

Then, to top it all, we received in our headquarters a taunting letter from an Islamite terrorist group that calls herself "The Mahdi's Emissaries". In this letter they claimed that they have managed to destroy our project! We are not sure of the truth of their claim. What we do know is that a terrible explosion, apparently caused by Anti-Matter, had destroyed both caves despite their spatial separation. We do not know if the explosion was accidental, or caused by a terrorist's sabotage act, as the letter claimed. Either way, the tragic fact remains that the project is lost with all its people!!!

We questioned several intelligence services in the world and learned that the "Mahdi's emissaries" is a small Shiite terrorist group based in Iran. They are affiliated with the larger terrorist organization of Daesh ("the Islamic State of Iraq and the Levant"). They, like Daesh, believe in the Shiite doctrine of the imminent coming of the "day of judgment". They maintain that before this "day of judgment", an apocalypse will rock the world – a sort of "Armageddon". However, all the Muslims in the world will live and lead happy lives. Therefore, they believe that the climate's calamities that we are experiencing is this Armageddon. They also believe that a "messiah", called the "Imam Mahdi," will come in the "day of judgement", and will transform Islam into the only religion in the world. Therefore. they explained in their letter, they needed to preserve the Climate's apocalypse by destroying the devilish "Noah's Ark" proposal.

Here is the text of the letter, after a correction of its many style- and spelling mistakes:

La Allah ela Allah, wa Muhammad Rasul Allah (there is no God, but Allah, and Muhammad is his prophet)!

Heretic dogs, you tried to prevent the coming of the Mahdi by fighting the Climate's apocalypse. But we, Allah's believers, succeeded in foiling your evil proposal! You enlisted qualified miners and controlled exploders for your villainous project. We saw the chance that Allah created for us and sent you a bomber Shaheed whose name is "Saif el Islam" (the sword of Islam). (A shaheed is the term applied to those who sacrifice their lives for Allah's cause). We shall not divulge his real name since he still has a family in one of the western countries in which he grew up. "Saif el Islam" passed all your classification tests, including the Polygraph test. To pass this test, we told him to put a stone in his shoe. This will cause him a lot of pain and will distract his mind from the lies that he will have to tell! We have learned this trick by watching your corrupt television.

As an experienced miner and explosion expert, Saif el Islam had a free access to the explosives' storage room. We assume that he had found a chance and exploded a part of the cave in which the demonic Anti-Matter was produced. We do not know exactly how he carried out his heroic mission. But when we read your announcement that an extremely large explosion ruined you project, we knew that he succeeded in his mission. He is now in heaven under the care of Allah, being served by 72 beautiful maidens who cater to all his requests.

Ya'eesh (long live) the Mahdi, blessed be all the believers and death to all heretic dogs!

It is quite possible that the small terrorist group of the "Mahdi's Emissaries" falsely took credit of the explosion to enlist more terrorists into their rows. Before the issuing of the present announcement, we approached all the leaders of the free world and asked them to fix a Global Day of Mourning in memory of the dead heroes. All of them agreed, and the day chosen is 11.23.2024. Please honor the project's victims by standing for a minute of silence. May our dead heroes rest in peace!!!

A notice to the first relatives of the dead heroes (husbands, wives, brothers, sisters, and parents):

Our hearts bleed for your loss. On our part, we can supply you only with a very small consolation: We shall immediately transfer to you all the monetary compensations due to your dead relatives – Life insurance payment, the (forced) end of work benefit, and you will be entitled to all the retirement pensions of your relatives, throughout your life. If you wish it, we shall also send you expert psychologists that may help you during your mourning period.

We have all your contact addresses, and we shall call you very soon. Those of you that we were unable to contact due to a change of address, are asked to phone the organization's headquarters in Washington (202-376 6704/5/6) or write an e-mail (noah@org.corp). Our offices will stay open for another year and our accountants will do their utmost to assist you.

Please note this is the last announcement that will be issued by "Noah's Ark's" organization. As a result of the failure of proposal 6, the Ad-hoc emergency proposal no. 7 will go into effect, as promised to you by the Bill Just and Walt Beaufort. The personnel of proposal No. 7 will help all refugees in the world from now on and will issue new contact addresses that will answer any cry for help.

Goodbye and good luck to all of you from me, the grieving **John Roberts**

Operations' Diary of John Roberts
(Top Secret and Private)

02.05.2028

Dear Diary,

To my great surprise, while overwhelmed with grief, I received a Skype call today from the "netherworld". I was in my office, completing the last details in the "burial" of "**Noah's Ark**" and the transfer of files to Proposal No. 7's Tycoons. Just's and Beaufort's assets and money were already transferred to the tycoons according to wills that my bosses wrote a long time ago and left with an executor of the wills that they chose.

At first, I thought that a stray old Skype's broadcast was inserted by mistake into my computer. Then a second later, Bill Just's visage on the screen laughed and he re-introduced himself! I almost fell from my chair and did not join Bill's laughter at what seemed to him a like a big joke. I immediately understood and filled with relief, I still scolded him for the mourning that he caused me to undergo! Bill Just apologized profusely and then said that the caves were not destroyed and that when I shall come to the caves, he will tell me the reason for the lie that he and Beaufort perpetrated on the world. He also ordered me to take Anna, Jeanie, and our children and to come discreetly and quickly to the caves. Jeanie's children were already staying in the caves. Bill told me to take the train from Washington to Kennedy airport where Beaufort's private plane is parked. We shall fly to Sochi, and from there we and the plane's pilots and their families will be transported to the caves at night.

I performed Bill Just's request and after about twenty hours, all of us reached the caves undetected. For the first time since I joined the Noah's Ark organization, I had a chance to see the monumental enterprise that I described to the whole world …

BOOK 3

THE CAT IS OUT
OF THE BAG

CHAPTER 9

The Sanctuary

The Lord then said to Noah, "Go into the ark, you and your whole family. Seven days from now I will send rain on the earth for forty days and forty nights, and I will wipe from the face of the earth every living creature I have made." In the six hundredth year of Noah's life, on the seventeenth day of the second month—on that day all the springs of the great deep burst forth, and the floodgates of the heavens were opened. The waters rose and increased greatly on the earth, and the ark floated on the surface of the water. They rose greatly on the earth, and all the high mountains under the entire heavens were covered.

Excerpts from Genesis, chapter 7 of the Old Testament

Meanwhile in the caves, since the jobs of the building of the camp and the installation of the Cyclotrons and their accessories had been completed, the workers could rest and enjoy all the educational, recreational and sports facilities of the camp. They were happy that the production of Anti-Matter was proceeding well and waited for the solution of the packaging project. Finally, uninterrupted by the work shifts, they could enjoy long nights' sleep. The exception to that leisure, were the physicists who continued to work feverishly on the bothersome problem of the packaging.

The workers who were not employed in the **Anti-Matter** production labs, started to pack their belonging in anticipation for their flight to their homes. Those who had no homes to return to, knew that the Noah's Ark's consortium will supply them new homes. All of them also waited in anticipation to draw the salaries that were saved for them in banks back home and to receive all the severance benefits were promised to them.

Then, on 02.15.2028, when the workers woke up and tried to read their E-mails, or to talk with their relatives on Skype, they saw the following notice:

"Dear friends,

It is not possible at present to open connections to the outside world. An explanation for the stoppage will be provided to all of you, in a general meeting in the assembly hall/theater that will take place today at 10:00 AM. The participation of all workers, their spouses, and their older children is obligatory!'"

Signed: Bill Just and Walt Beaufort

The notice caused heated discussions among the workers who came out of their huts to dredge up information from their neighbors. Such a stoppage event and a call to a general workers' meeting, had never happened before! Most of the workers assumed that in the general meeting they will receive instructions on the coming transport homes. Other thought that it is going to be a start of celebrations on their successful completion of all the cave's requirements. Others, more philosophically minded, waited patiently for 10:00 O'clock.

The riddle was solved when a diligent worker by the name of Bob Klein, who oversaw the safe operation of all elevators in the caves, performed an unscheduled safety inspection. When he came to the Kyubishevskaya's entrance elevator, he was shocked to find that the ascent of the elevator was stopped several scores of feet from the top. He tried to open the escape hatch in the top of the elevator's car by force and found that it was stuck. All his attempts only yielded a falling drizzle of sand and pebbles. In a great panic, he descended, and ran to Krubera's entrance elevator and found the same result!

Breathless, and with eyes almost popping out from their sockets, he ran to the public address system of the Kyubishevskaya's camp and cried: "help! Help! Both entrances to the outside had collapsed, the elevators are stuck, and we are completely cut off from the world!" when Bob completed his message, immediate chaos has erupted. The men remained silent and turned pale, while the women and children cried in in terror!

Within seconds, Beaufort ran to the public address system and cried: "Please, please, relax all of you! We are not in danger! Our Safety engineer, John Britten, initiated an emergency simulation of an avalanche by small explosions in our entrances. We wanted to stress the importance of corrective actions that should be applied in case of a real disaster. He was supposed to instruct you what to do in case of a real emergency today in the 10:00 meeting!

Our over-diligent Bob Klein "jumped the gun" when he carried out an unscheduled inspection of the elevators. His weekly inspection is due only two days from now. We beg your forgiveness for the deception! We should have anticipated the risk of an untimely discovery!" The workers and their families finally calmed down after some protest-muttering and returned to their huts.

At the assigned time, all the workers and their families, except for those who had to care for babies and young children, or were busy at the dining hall, assembled in the meeting hall/ theatre. On the stage sat Just, Beaufort and the six leaders of the work groups. At a back of the stage hung a large banner with the emblem of the "Noah's Ark" organization.

Bill Just stood up, went to the microphone, tapped on it to assure himself that it is working properly, and said:

"Dear friends, you are already aware of the unfortunate simulation that we carelessly hurled at you. And you probably realize by now that all the communication to the outside world had been deliberately cut by us. Let me now reveal to you the real reason behind the simulation and the communication-stoppage. It was not really meant to instruct you on emergency safety means!" All present drew a deep breath and waited apprehensively for what Bill Just is going to say. Then he continued:

"The small blocking explosions that John Britten and some of his best men performed at our behest, are real, but not dangerous. We are not imprisoned since we can exit at any time we want! John Britten and his miners dug an escape tunnel in parallel to the blocked entrance in Kyubishevskaya and camouflaged its exit with dummy "wooden rocks". In addition, we can easily drill back a way through the blockage.

The purpose of all the work was to deceive everyone **in the outside world** and make them believe that the caves were destroyed by a huge, accidental, Anti-Matter explosion! For that purpose, we also blew up our communication tower. I will describe to you now the reason behind these deceptions:

As you know, we had promised the whole world that we are going to produce Anti-Matter, and in this, we indeed succeeded. However, we also promised humanity that we are working very hard on the problem of the packing of Anti-Matter into small bomblets, and that we are sure to succeed. Lin-Hua and her team are indeed working on the problem. However, they are stymied. The technology of packing of the Anti-Matter in small containers such as bomblets does not exist yet, and it may take several years to solve the problem, and perhaps not even then.

I am sorry to say that Beaufort and I knew about this snag and have lied to the whole world and, may God forgive us, we have also deceived you! We did that because about two years ago we received an ominous warning from the climatologists of our organization that our world is **soon going to perish. "In less than two years from now"**, they said, **"the whole world is going to be flooded by ocean water and huge rains that will swamp all habitable areas except for the mountaintops!"** This will happen because of a rapid heating of our oceans that is already in progress and thaws all the glaciers around the world. Such a massive thaw had already

started some years ago and is now **rapidly accelerating.**
Moreover, we are going to be attacked by **unstopping very
heavy rains.**

In a minute, I am going to let Dr. Green, who is our chief
climatologist, and substitutes as the science teacher in our high
school, to describe why this apocalypse is coming. He will
also explain how he, and his colleagues at our organization,
reached the ominous conclusion that our world is quickly
dying.

This conclusion caused Beaufort and me to deceive you
and all Humanity. As a result, proposal No. 6 should now be
called proposal No. 6A! **The purpose of the new proposal
6A is to establish a viable nucleus of humanity. Some of
you and all your descendants will be able, eventually,
to return to a dry earth after the flood, and restart the
propagation of Humanity.** Again, I humbly beg your
forgiveness. At least you will be saved, and I believe that, in
time, you will forgive us! As for our deception of the whole
world, our act is unforgivable, and Beaufort and I shall carry
this guilt, as a Mark of Cain on our foreheads for as long as
we live!" Here, Just, with tears in his eyes, relinquished his
place near the microphone to Dr. Green. All present sat in
silence and awe and waited for Dr. Green's words.

Dr. Green started:

"Dear friends,

At the start of my address, I want to say that I respect and admire all of you for the hard work that you invested in our common project. As Bill said, because of our failure with the packaging of the **Anti-Matter,** we must accept our chairmen's **proposal 6A,** or else perish together with all humanity. I believe that since we have a chance to survive, we must accept it for the sake of our families, but much more than that – **for the sake of the future of humanity**!

Now, let me digress a little; I want to ask both you and me, an "existentialistic" rhetorical question: Do we have a right to a fresh start in a post-flood Earth? Remember that in the past, Humanity corrupted our Earth's climate with greenhouse gases. Parts of Humanity exploited various nations, started wars that caused the death of millions, nurtured racism, and let our fellowmen starve in Africa and elsewhere. Moreover, one so-called "cultural" nation, exterminated members of other nations and 2 race: Jews and gypsies, by gassing and burning in crematoria!

To answer this rhetorical question, I can answer emphatically that **we do, indeed, have the right to survive and resuscitate Humanity!** We shall be turning loose upon a post-flood virgin Earth **good, idealistic people!** Without your knowledge, Professor Dumas and her team screened all of you, genetically, for an existence of the "warrior gene," a gene in the X chromosome of males or a reduced- size-Amygdala in the brain. The existence of these 2 traits, or even just one of them leads to murderous flare-ups and criminal tendencies in their carriers. None of these traits were found in your genomes, or in your brains. In addition, Professor Evans and his team of psychologists screened all applicants and **chose you,** because of your strong tendency towards altruism, kind heart and the ability to like and honor persons from other cultures, races, and skin color.

Yes! We are good people, both genetically and psychologically, and I think that we deserve the right to populate a new Earth!" All the workers listened intently, liking the praises that were heaped on them.

"Now I shall come to our present predicament. The catastrophe that we are facing is here to stay for quite a long time and will not relent! Observations that had been going on for several generations by many climatologists, have defined an extremely important factor, **additional to that of the greenhouse gases**, that influences our climate - **Sunspots!** Sunspots are short-lived phenomena in the Sun's photosphere (external surface layer) that appear as areas darker than their surrounding areas. They are regions of reduced surface temperature, caused by fluctuations of the magnetic field of the sun.

Sunspots repeatedly appear according to an 11-year-**cycle.** They expand and contract as they move across the surface of the Sun, with diameters ranging from 10 miles to 100,000 miles. The larger varieties of the sunspots are visible from Earth, even without the aid of a telescope. Resulting from an intense magnetic activity of the sun, **the receding end of the sunspots are accompanied by other solar phenomena such as solar flares and sun-burst-ejections into space.** The sunspots stay for a few months and then disappear until a new 11-year cycle of sunspots arrives. Although the sunspots are colder than that of the unspotted sun's surface area, in end of the 11-year cycle of sunspots, the **unspotted areas, as I already told you previously,** becomes hotter than the usual sun's temperature. During this time, the oceans and soil on our earth **do heat-up,** but **only slightly**.

However, aside from the 11-year cycles that I described, there are also additional cycles, called the **Wolf-Gleissberg** cycles., These cycles recur about every 100 years (that is after each 9 or 10 eleven-year cycles).

The Sun's warming at the end of a 100-year-Wolf-Gleissberg cycle, is greater than that appears in the end of an 11-year cycle, **but even this cycle is not hot enough to exterminate all humanity.** However, this is not the end of the story of our Sun's repeating sunspots and flare-ups! At the end of 10 Wolf-Gleissberg cycles, that is, at the end of every thousand years, there is yet **another, warmer flare-up, that is still only mildly dangerous.** However, at the end of each ten[th] thousand-year **Wolf-Gleissberg's cycle, a huge "end-of-the-world" catastrophe takes place.** The sun becomes **much warmer and "attacks" our planet very vigorously.** Unfortunately, there is nothing that can be done about it. It is a rule of nature! The last "end of the world" catastrophe that had occurred in the past, had left an echo in the mythologies of several ancient nations, as I shall soon describe.

All the climatologists in our dying world are familiar with the ten-thousand-year effect of the Wolf-Gleissberg cycle. However, they are not overly concerned, because several pieces of evidence have shown that it is just the **fourth 1000 cycle** that is about to end. In other words, only **4000** years had passed from the last **"planet busting"** climatological event. **Unfortunately, these placid climatologists did not consider the effect of the greenhouse gases that did not exist in the past but do now. They are** transforming the **fourth** thousand-cycle **to a tenth-thousand -cycle planet-busting event!!!**

Soon, (within 2 years, according to our computers' prediction), all the continents in our world will be flooded with10 to 15 meter of ocean water because of the accelerating thawing of all the ice in our world and the continuous heavy rains. Only mountaintops will be free of flood- and rainwater. Those populations who will flee to high mountains, will not lack fresh drinking water, because of heavy rains that will constantly fall. However, these rains will inhibit food production, and the poor refugees will soon perish of starvation.

Some temporary exception to this tragic end will be the populations of rice-growing countries such as Vietnam,

China, Thailand, Korea, and other countries of Southeast Asia. This is because rice is grown in water-swamped fields that exist in valleys between high mountains and their slopes. However, even these valleys and slopes will finally sink under water, and its inhabitants will also succumb to starvation.

For quite some time I, and some others of my colleagues had studied the stories of ancient cultures to determine if, and when, there had been climatic catastrophes in the past. We found that myths about **a worldwide flood** had appeared in traditions of several ancient cultures: the Acadian, Sumerian, Babylonian, Greek, Irish, Indian, Chinese, Indonesian, Polynesian, Mayan, Incan, Aztecan, and several other cultures. According to these myths, the **last** 10th- millennium- Wolf-Gleissberg's cycle had ended about **4000** years ago with a huge worldwide flood.

One of the more interesting myths (whose origin is very ancient), came from India. According to this myth, the world is destroyed and is recreated **in cycles,** and each cycle of destruction comes in the wake of a great, inevitable moral deterioration. After each such cycle of destruction, a golden egg floats on top of the floodwater, carrying the sleeping Creator God Brahma. When Brahma wakes up, he remembers his past creations, comes out of the egg, and re-creates the world ...

In addition, I want to mention that diggings in the ancient Sumerian cities of Ur, Kish, and Assur, revealed signs of a flood that happened 2000 years BC - that is about **4000 years ago**. This proves that we are now chronologically at the end of the **fourth** Wolf-Gleissberg cycle. However, as I mentioned before, the end of this cycle, **together with the greenhouse gases, spells an End-of-the-World Catastrophe**!

Finally, I want to describe another myth, a Mesopotamian one, that also found its way into the "**Noah's Ark's**" story of the Old Testament. This myth is called "the epic of Gilgamesh, king of Uruk." The epic is one of the most ancient literary works – dating from the third Ur period, that is about 2000 years BC (about **4000** years ago!). According to one of the chapters of the epic, two gods, Anu, the father of the gods, and Enlil, God of earth, wind, and air, planned to bring a flood to the world and destroy all humanity. This plan arose as the result of the fact that humans made a lot of noise that interfered with the 2 Gods slumber…

But Ea, the goddess of wisdom, revealed to Utnapishtim, the king of Uruk, of the impending flood. She counseled him to build a boat in which he, his family, and the pairs of every living animal will be able to escape. This he did, and after twelve days of floating, he opened the hatch of his boat and saw the slopes of Mount Nisir (Ararat of the Old Testament). On the seventh day of the boat's landing on Mount Nisir, Utnapishtim sent a dove out to see if the water had receded. The dove found only water all over and returned. Then he sent out a swallow, and just as before, it returned. Finally,

Utnapishtim sent out a raven, and the raven saw that the waters had receded, and did not return. Utnapishtim then released all the animals from the boat and made a sacrifice to the gods.

There are similarities between the story of Utnapishtim, and that of Noah and his Ark in the Old Testament: the first similarity is that there is a divine decision to bring a flood to kill every living thing on earth. But one righteous person, warned by a God, saved himself and his family and pairs of all animals. The second similarity is the sending of a dove and the sacrifices after the rescue. However, the reason for the flood in the epic of Gilgamesh is not the corruption of humanity, but the ire of the two major gods, Anu and Enlil, whose sleep had been interrupted by the humans, as I already described...

I cannot forecast **when** the climate will improve. However, because of the Wolf-Gleissberg cyclicality that I described above, I estimate that the flood and rainfalls will stop after 100 years, and a "virgin" Earth will be exposed. As a result, I believe that our descendants in the future will be able to search for new "Atlantises" such as New London, New Moscow, etc.

Thanks to the far-reaching tragic, decisions of our chairmen, we shall survive the flood. Our descendants, who will emerge from our sanctuary, equipped with treasures of knowledge, will be able to re-populate earth successfully.

This is all that I planned to say today. Thank you for your attentiveness and bless you all".

Beaufort now approached the microphone and said: "Dear 'Terranaout" travelers,

Finally, the moment had come for Bill, Dr. Green, Professor Lin-Hua Chen, and me, to confess about the sins that we have carried alone for too long: - the deceptions that we perpetrated on all of you, but most importantly, on all humanity! As already mentioned by Bill, since announcement No. 15, we have all been engaged in **Proposal No. 6A, "the sanctuary proposal**." In our defense, I must say that with great vigor and good faith, we initiated all our six proposals. When the first five proposals failed, we still hoped that Professor Chen, against all odds, will succeed with the packaging problem, and that we shall be able save the world. However, when she concluded that she would need much more time to solve the packaging problem, proposal No. **6A** became inevitable! My heart bleeds for all the drowning billions, but we must continue **alone with proposal 6A** for the sake of a quick resuscitation of humans after the flood.

Several Fantasy writers wrote imaginative books based on the idea that all humanity almost perished because of ancient floods during history. They claimed, (quite justifiably!) that ancient thriving cultures, which had almost completely perished, were responsible for marvelous artifacts that are found in our world. The list of artifacts is long, but I shall mention only a few of them - the Sphinx in Egypt, the Mayan pyramid in Tikal Guatemala, and the Stonehenge in Britain.

Many candidates tried to join our enterprise. But only you, a few hundred out of several thousand, were chosen.

As Dr. green had hinted, we had established several physiological and psychological parameters for acceptance. Some of these parameters were briefly mentioned by Dr. Green. The list that I shall soon enumerate, will illustrate what kind of persons we needed for the resuscitation of humanity after the deluge. These parameters were also tested in your spouses and girl- or boyfriends who wanted to join you. We apologize for performing these tests, because they smack of the eugenic selection plan of the type that Hitler exercised against the Jews, homosexuals, psychiatric patients, and gypsies. Our only excuse is that we needed mentally- and physically- healthy "Terranauts" for the re-settlement of our world. Here is the list of the selection parameters:

1. The strength of your ties to the outside world. Either that you do not have close relatives at all, or that you had been out of touch with them for years.
2. The absence of genes which are responsible for serious diseases such as Huntington's, Dwarfism, and Epilepsy.
3. An absence of chronic Viruses, such HIV, Corona-viruses and Hepatitis viruses.

4. The absence of genes that may cause various types of Cancers, such as Breast- and Ovary-, and Digestive tract cancers.

5. Complete absence of any tendency for claustrophobia (therefore you spent several hours in a narrow, closed, and dark isolation cell).

6. Lack of Alzheimer's disease incidence in your older relatives.

7. The absence of any genetic markers that will cause murderous flare-ups in their carriers.

On the other hand, we examined you for the presence of:

- A procreative ability of both members of the applying families and in single applicants

- A high intelligence, (for that you were tested in various IQ questionnaires).

- A genetic propensity for empathy and cooperativeness.

I believe that some of you may resent the fact that we forced on you a mode of "life-long prison life" without consulting you. However, those among you who wish to return to the doomed world will be able to leave through the camouflaged substitute entrance. We shall transport them secretly to Sochi Airport in buses with strong engines that we saved from destruction. They will take you through the strong winds on

Arabica to Sochi. We will also supply you with travel money and money for housing.

Please confer with your families and make up your minds within 48 hours, since we are pressed for time. If you leave, our accountants will compensate you with all the payments and benefits that were promised to you when you enlisted. Those who are leaving, must solemnly promise that they will never reveal what happened in the "exploded" caves. We shall trust their promises, because we know that they will not expose their friends to the danger of invasion and murder by flood-fugitives. Also, after they leave, we ask them not to return to their previous houses if they still exist. If by any chance, they will be recognized in their new locations, they should claim that they do not know what happened during the "explosion," since they left early, when they completed their assignments.

Those of you and your spouses, who are going to stay in the sanctuary, would not remain idle. Besides the daily survival chores such as cooking, the tending of the hydroponic gardens, the fishpond, the cowshed, and looking after your families, all of you will perform additional functions. These will be **the cataloging of all your specialist expertise.**

Mrs. Schwabé hired librarians and information experts for our enterprise. While our Internet was still operating, they recorded many classical, religious, and contemporary musical works and songs, as well as many literary masterpieces. They also photographed works of art, sculptures, and paintings from many centuries and a lot of data from physics-, medical-, and biological books. This had turned our store of knowledge into something like the huge ancient Library in Alexandria, Egypt ... As you may know, perhaps, the ancient library of Alexandria was the biggest and most important library in the Hellenistic period. It contained every manuscript that was available at that time - almost 700,000 parchment scrolls. It was established in 288 BC by king Ptolemius the first and for several centuries it was the largest reservoir of knowledge in the ancient world. Between the 4th and the 7th centuries AC several big fires destroyed the library. It is claimed that the fires were lit by Christians who considered the scrolls to be pagan.

Each one of you will have to assimilate skills and experience from tapes and other information media and from one or two or specialists from areas different than your current skills. We intend that for every single expert there will be one or more additional substitute specialist.

Finally, you probably know that Bill Just and I brought our families to the sanctuary. However, despite our families' objections, Just and I decided to leave the sanctuary and join the drowning populations because of our great sin!"

A complete hush enveloped everybody in the meeting hall, and everybody waited for Beaufort's words: "As Bill had already told you, we have developed proposals 1 to 6 with the help of the organization's scientists in the real hope that at least one proposal will succeed. Unfortunately, all that we managed to achieve was **the big deception of proposal 6A – this sanctuary**! Therefore, Bill and I had decided to pay the penalty for our deception by joining humanity's demise. As Bill already told you, we cannot hide in the safety the sanctuary, thinking of all the billions of people that we lied to! To replace us, Bill and I recommend that you appoint Dr. Green as the new chairmen of the sanctuary, subject to your agreement."

A general pandemonium erupted in the meeting hall, with everybody shouting protests and denials. Roberts snatched the microphone from Beaufort's hands and exclaimed: "Bill, Walt, your sacrificial act is impossible! We need you!

Dr. Green took the microphone from Roberts and cried: "Dear Chairmen, I am sure that I speak in the name of all of us in this meeting hall when I demand that you renounce your senseless decision!" Then, addressing the audience he said: "Friends, let us block this noble and irresponsible act of our bosses! Imprison them gently right now! They will be freed only after world's end. We still need their leadership and counsel in the years to come"!

All the sanctuary's residents clapped hands in agreement, and several husky masons grabbed the struggling chairmen, locked them in an unoccupied hut, and guarded every possible point of escape. The guards supplied food to the prisoners and took turns in the cleaning of the hut, and in doing the prisoners' laundry. At the start, the prisoners tried to persuade the guards to free them, but finally gave up. Possibly, they were even happy that they were forced to stay alive. After a time in prison, when it became obvious that they will not be able to leave the sanctuary, they were released and returned to manage the sanctuary.

During the first 48 hours after their imprisonment, Beaufort and Just waited impatiently for a report from Mrs. Schwabé on the number of people and families who decided to leave the sanctuary. They calmed down only when they learned that their number was small.

Operations' Diary of John Roberts
(Top Secret and Private)

22.22.2024

Dear Diary,

after watching the proceedings of the last week, my admiration for Just and Beaufort increased tremendously. Almost like Chess grand masters, they predicted the necessary steps that should be taken if the six "Noah's Ark" proposals will fail. Also, as enterprising businessmen, they acted ruthlessly to carry out the sanctuary proposal. My admiration was also influenced by the gratitude that I felt for their saving my family, and most of all, for giving humanity a fresh start in a "brave new world." Even more than that, I respected their honorable attempt to with the perishing of Humanity!

BOOK 4

A "A BRAVE NEW WORLD"

Chapter 10

"be fruitful, and multiply upon the earth"

"In the six hundredth and first year, in the first month, the first day of the month, the waters were dried up from off the earth and Noah removed the covering of the ark, and looked, and behold, the face of the ground was dry. And in the second month, on the seven and twentieth day of the month, was the earth dried And God spake unto Noah, saying Go forth of the ark, thou, and thy wife, thy sons, and thy sons' wives with thee that they may breed abundantly in the Earth, and Be fruitful, and multiply upon the earth"

Excerpt from Genesis, chapter 8 of the Old Testament

T he sanctuary's residents and their descendants waited for 40 years in their sanctuary until the sea waters stopped rising. Next, they had to wait for the sun to evaporate the high seas and when normal winter temperatures returned, they waited for the re-freezing of glaciers all over the world and the drying of the flood waters. This process had taken 60 additional years, and allowed the sanctuary's residents to exit finally, after 100 long years from their home. The population in the caves increased only slightly during those 100 years. Since space was scarce inside the sanctuary, by common assent, they refrained from reproduction.

Below see the table arranged by our statistician:

Time duration	Alive	Age range	Deceased
Start of proposal No. 6A	1021	1 month – 55 years	0
First 30 years in the caves	1292	1 month – 85 years	25
The total time in the sanctuary until the ability to leave (100 years)	1323	1 month – 85 years	210
The start of the colonization (year 100th)	1401	1 month – 89 years	253

Some births were permitted if the prospective parents compensated for bringing a baby to the closed sanctuary by carving (with the help of mason friends) a space-increase from the walls of Kyubishevskaya.

After the evaporation of the seawater in the high range near the sanctuary, the sanctuary's residents waited five more years for the drying out of at least part of the area.

They selected from the drying areas, a zone encompassing a perimeter of 300 miles, in which they intended to build, with time, several colonies. During these five years of waiting, few young couples left the sanctuary and built temporary shelters near the sanctuary to live in, and to start having babies. They continued to use the sanctuary for food and medical support for their babies.

To survey the 300-mile perimeter that will be chosen, the sanctuary's residents sent a "dove" every 6 months. However, their "dove" was not of flesh and blood as in Noah's story, but a multirotor drone equipped with a sophisticated camera that sent back videos from the surveyed areas. The drone also contained an instrument that could measure the degree of salinity of the soil, with the intention of finding suitable agricultural lots whose salt was already washed away by rains.

A soon as the "dove" transmitted the location for a plot that contained the least amount of residual salinity for a first agricultural colony, all the sanctuary's residents decided, unanimously, to leave the sanctuary. Since the nearby Black Sea teemed with all sorts of fish and seafood species, the survivors established a fishing colony near the caves that supplied them with very nutritious food, in addition to the hydroponic garden.

Since the sanctuary's residents planned to colonize earth, they adopted a new name for themselves —"colonists." On their exit from the sanctuary, several "colonists" even bent down and joyfully kissed the soil. The descendants of the original sanctuary's clergymen tried to organize thanks-giving ceremonies in the hope of attracting the colonists back to religion but failed. Most colonists had lost their faith because of the death of billions of innocent victims in the flood.

When the colonists watched the videos that were sent by the "Dove" before their exit from the sanctuary, they could hardly believe their eyes. They expected to see a desolate planet completely devoid of any sign of life. However, even in the early videos, they could see a planet teeming with both fauna and flora. The flora consisted of plants that apparently adapted themselves to grow in shallow salt water on the high mountains. This they probably did by developing a reverse-osmosis mechanism in their roots that got rid of salts. Therefore, when the time came for migration from the sanctuary, the colonists released their cows and their bull and sent them to graze near the proposed colony and to multiply. The cattle stayed close to the caves and supplied milk for the new babies that were born to the young temporary-shelter couples.

The Fauna that the colonists saw in their videos, consisted mostly of herbivorous mountain dwellers such as Ibexes, Chinchillas, Hyraxes, Llamas, and Jerboas. The colonists were sorry to see that all birds and poultry, that could not fly high enough to reach the high mountains, were now extinct. Only high-flying predatory birds, such as Buzzards, falcons, hawks, and kites survived by feeding on carcasses of the rodents described above.

The "brave new world" that the colonists reclaimed, was free of various flying insects, and the colonists realized that any fruit trees that they were going to plant, could not be pollinated because of the absence of bees. However, the colonists consoled themselves that, at least, they would not be bothered any more by insects. The agricultural colony that they set up, eventually supplied them with various cereals. However, first they had to dedicate their first harvests to build large stocks of seeds. The "seed master" that Iris originally recruited, had died in the sanctuary. However, he transferred all his stocks of seeds and his knowledge to his daughter. Before the release from the sanctuary, the daughter germinated seeds of various trees that she intended to plant near the new agricultural colony.

The Krubera cave contained a cemetery that was visited by the sanctuary's residents during their life in the caves. Before their migration from the caves, the colonists built a tall monument near Krubera's entrance that carried a plaque honoring Bill Just and Walt Beaufort who passed away before the migration.

To help in the building of their new colonies, the colonists stripped the sanctuary all the important equipment and materials. They even dismantled several prefabricated huts to build homes quickly for the older colonists and the children.

The salvaged equipment also contained generators, computers, school equipment and much more. To transfer all the stores and equipment to the agricultural and fishing colonies, the colonists hitched carts to trucks and tractors that had been stored in a camouflaged, water-proof garage near the caves.

Chapter 11

New colonies and new settlers

Then God blessed Noah and his sons, saying to them, "Be fruitful and increase in number and fill the earth. 2 The fear and dread of you will fall on all the beasts of the earth, and on all the birds in the sky, on every creature that moves along the ground, and on all the fish in the sea; they are given into your hands. 3 Everything that lives and moves about will be food for you. Just as I gave you the green plants, I now give you everything

Excerpt from Genesis, chapter 9 of the Old Testament

The agricultural colony and the fishing site soon thrived and demonstrated how proficient the new colonists were because of all the knowledge that they have received from their parents and "uncles"/"aunts" during their life in the sanctuary. Not many remained from the original sanctuary's residents and those that did, had to be very young when they entered the caves with their parents. As already described above, he younger progeny of the sanctuary's residents chose mates when they were still in the sanctuary, and when all procreation restrictions were removed in the new colonies, they happily did their share to extend the colonists' number.

All the colonists who were proficient in the various building skills, such as Masons, carpenters, roadbuilders, plumbers, air-condition experts, as well as cooks, agronomists, and the operators of electric power stations, were the ones who mostly did the work of the building of the new agricultural and fishing colonies. The electrical power generators that the colonists brought with them did not use gas fuel, since they operated with **Anti-Matter** capsules. Such capsules of various sizes were finally produced by Professor Lin-Hua Chen about 10 years in the caves.

The colonists intended that, with the increase in their numbers, large groups would be able to leave the original two colonies to establish a chain of new colonies. They hoped that the colonies will eventually become new cities, to "replenish the earth". They were careful to maintain a great genetic variety in their colonies. That is why they decreed that each new group colonists that to build a new colony, would have to start with many colonists. They also recommended that young colonists would search their mates in colonies other than their own, and, eventually, in other cities, to achieve genetic variety.

Learning from the history of a divided earth, the colonists vowed to quench any quarrels between future colonies, and future cities, and to remain united nation. They even adopted the traditional moto of the United States: "E Pluribus Unum" - "out of many one." Moreover, they also decided to maintain a single universal language that was to be English. Nevertheless, they did not to stop any colonist who wanted to study the original language of his ancestors from the sanctuary's library, but in addition to his knowledge of English.

When the building of the first new agricultural- and the first fishing colonies were completed and the sea and the virgin soil yielded excellent harvests, the colonists threw a big party, feasting on products from their new colonies. They were happy to be alive in a free and a peacefull world that they fashioned for themselves.

Chapter 12

New technics and new inventions

s long as the colonies were under accelerated building, and seeding regimen, the descendants of the sanctuary's scientists served as apprentices to the masons, carpenters, and agronomists. Anyway, all their scientific equipment, including that used to produce **Anti-Matter,** remained in the caves. However, as little by little, the pressure of the building and agricultural work had diminished, the scientists were liberated a little and drove from time to time to the sanctuary to manage their laboratories, the Cyclotrons, and their accessories.

The scientists waited impatiently for the time when they would be asked to produce and to pack it in containers of various sizes as they had learned some 50 years ago from Professor Li-Hua Chen. During the building of the sanctuary in proposal 6, the sanctuary's residents drew expensive electricity from a

Russian electrical power station. Under Proposal 6A, when they hid in the sanctuary, they produced electricity with gas turbine generators. The gas had been liquefied under high pressure into containers that the sanctuary's residents had imported to the caves. Luckily, before all the gas was exhausted, Professor Chen finally found a solution to the **anti-Matter** packaging problem.

According to the life history of the sanctuary, which was written by one of the information specialists, Bill Just summoned a special meeting about 10 years after the enclosure in the caves to distribute the news of the solution achieved by Li-Hua. He opened the meeting by voicing his great regret that the solution was achieved too late and could not save Humanity. But he also expressed great joy on Professor Chen's achievement, and then he yielded the microphone to Li-Hua. Her address was reported verbatim in the sanctuary's history records.

Professor Chen said: "Dear friends, I am glad to see all of you gathered in a meeting, since it means that important news is to be divulged in it. The present meeting is convened to talk about **Anti-Matter**! as all of you know, any meeting of **Anti-Matter** with **Normal Matter**, including that of the packagings' **normal matter** casings, will cause a nullification of both **matters** with a release of a vast amount of energy. Until the start of the flood, in all the known studies, **Anti-Matter** could only be kept safely in special traps in which it hung in the middle of the traps. This "mid-hanging" was achieved with strong magnets. However, the mass of **Anti-Matter** that was imprisoned in such traps was small. This was because a greater mass of the positively charged **Anti-Matter positrons** repelled each other, so that they were pushed to the **Normal- Matter** walls of the packaging. Moreover, those packagings were large and could not be produced in the large numbers that were required to destroy the greenhouse gases.

After "hibernating" for 10 years, I hit upon a simple idea! This idea allowed me to store **positively charged Anti-Matter ions** inside a packaging of any size that I want, provided that the packaging will have an inside lining **ALSO** made from **positively charged, BUT Normal matter ions.** The positive **Anti-matter** and the positive **Normal matter** will strongly repel each other and will never meet! To produce positively charged **anti matter ions** I "bombed" the **Normal matter atoms of the packagings** with a stream of **positively charged anti-matter (positrons) from my cyclotron!** Thus, the **TWO positively charged materials**, one **Anti-matter** and one **normal mater** could live together in peace in any package that we want!

To those of you who do not know what **ions** are, let me explain: ions are electrically charged atoms formed by the **loss** or **gain** of one or more electrons from the atoms. A positive ion is created by an electron **loss**, whereas a negative ion is created by an electron **gain**. As you can see, sometimes there are simple solutions to problems that seemed unsolvable in the past. I chastise myself for not thinking about this simple solution early enough to save humanity!"

The history-record goes on to describe the happiness of the sanctuary's residents at hearing the news, because they knew that Lin-Hua's breakthrough, portended great success for their new enterprises on the "brave new world" of the future. Most of the sanctuary's residents also tried to console the grieving Lin-Hua, together with congratulating her on her great achievement.

As soon as more and more scientists among the colonists were released from their building bondage, the chemists among them also started to demonstrate their own expertise. They have developed new building materials for the masons. These materials were made of hollow nanotubes whose thickness was 50 nanometers and had a length of several microns. The chemists weaved the nanotubes into large, light, and long fabrics of extreme strength and duration. These fabrics could be molded into any shape that was needed. The weaving was performed in automatic looms that were produced for them by operators of computerized lathes.

Little by little, and then with greater speed, the colonists multiplied and built new colonies and cities in their new fertile earth. At the beginning of each year, depending on the time zone, the colonists held a memorial ceremony for the nation's great historical heroes - Bill Just and Walt Beaufort.

In these yearly ceremonies, they glorified their memory and recounted the great adventure that their ancestors underwent with their chairmen in the sanctuary. Let us all also bless their memories!

The end

ABOUT THE AUTHOR

The author obtained an M. Sc. Degree in Microbiology from the University of Tel-Aviv and a Ph.D. degree in microbiology from the University of Pennsylvania's Medical School.

Later he worked several years in the Virology institute of the St. Louis University. He has always been interested in Science fiction and had published 3 SF novels. He lives in Tel-aviv and is married, has 2 sons and 3 grandsons.

Printed in the United States
by Baker & Taylor Publisher Services